Dear Julie and Rob!

Meeting both of you has been
a profound blessing in my life.
From the depths of my heart,
I extend my sincerest gratitude
for your unwavering belief in me
and for supporting "Letters of Love."

Our mutual bond, strengthened
through the boundless grace of
Jesus Christ, is a testament to
His divine presence in our lives.

Sharing this profound connection
and delighting together in the
grace of ou Savior is genuinely
extraordinary.
May "Letters of Love" be a beacon
of encouragement and blessings
for you. I am deeply honored by
your decision to dive into its
pages and I hope it resonates
with the same love and faith
we cherish together.
With LOVE ♡ Sylvia Mills

Letters of Love

By Sylwia Mills

Examples of Letters From Blossoming
Romance To Deeply Devoted Christian Love

Letters of Love

Examples of Letters from Blossoming Romance to Deeply Devoted Christian Love

By

Sylwia Mills

Copyright

First Edition

Case id: 1-12695275791

ISBN: 978-1-4467-8697-0

Published by The Writers Tree.

Illustrations by Sylwia Mills

Printed in the United States

Dedication

To my beloved husband, Brad,
Your love, strength, and unwavering faith have been my constant source of inspiration. In your arms, I found solace and comfort, and in your heart, I have discovered a sanctuary of love. It is from this place of deep connection and shared devotion that the idea for this book was born.

A year ago, we embarked on a beautiful journey together—a tradition of writing love letters to one another. It was a transformative experience that brought forth a whirlwind of emotions and revealed the true power of words. Each letter became a reflection of our love, a testament to the depths of our feelings and a celebration of the beautiful bond we share.

This book is more than just a collection of letters; it is a tribute to the art of expressing love through the written words. It is a homage to the time-honored tradition of pouring out our hearts on paper, capturing the essence of our emotions, and preserving them for eternity.

It is a testament to the enduring power of love and a heartfelt letter's profound impact on the recipient.

But beyond the celebration of our love and the beauty of written expressions, this book is also a celebration of our journey—a journey not only with each other but with our Savior, Jesus Christ.

Our love is deeply rooted in our faith, and it is our unwavering devotion to Him that guides us through life's ups and downs. It is through our walk with Jesus that we find strength, peace, and endless inspiration to love one another unconditionally.

I dedicate this book to our Walk With Jesus—a journey that intertwines our love for each other and our love for our Savior. It is a dedication to the grace and guidance we have received along the way and the blessings that have been bestowed upon our relationship.

To all who read these pages, whether you are a believer or a skeptic, may this book serve as an inspiration to express your own feelings of love, to deepen your connections with those dear to you, and to cherish the love that fills your life.

May it gently encourage you to open your heart to the possibilities of love, to embrace vulnerability, and to let your words flow with sincerity and authenticity.

May your hearts always be filled with love, and may your words carry the power to touch the souls of others. Through the art of expressing love through letters, may you find joy, connection, and the everlasting magic of true love.
With all my love,
Sylwia Mills

About the Author

Sylwia's journey is a testament to her unwavering spirit and determination to pursue her dreams. Born in Brenna, Poland, she embarked on a courageous solo journey to Chicago, Illinois, with a fervent hope for the American dream.

Her remarkable journey caught the attention of many, and she was featured in magazine and newspaper articles for her achievements, including being crowned queen in the prestigious Legion of Young Polish Women's White and Red Ball. The Legion of Young Polish Women is an organization that annually celebrates Polish heritage and traditions, fostering unity and community among young Polish women.

While studying to become a registered nurse in America, Sylwia worked as a babysitter, displaying her unwavering work ethic, and commitment to her goals. Eventually, she obtained her nursing license and found her way to the enchanting shores of Miami, Florida, a place she had always dreamed of with its palm trees and warm climate. It was during this time that Sylwia's journey took on a deeper spiritual dimension, drawing her closer to her Lord Jesus Christ.

Having been raised Catholic in Poland, Sylwia had always held a deep reverence for God but had not fully realized the possibility of having a personal and intimate relationship with Jesus Christ. It was in Miami that she was shepherded in a gentle and nurturing way, guiding

her to discover the joy and depth of a personal relationship with her Savior and King.
As the Lord led Sylwia to the Fort Myers area, she encountered the love of her life, Brad Mills. Their connection was instant and profound, leading them to unite in marriage on a picturesque beach in Cape Coral just five months and ten days after meeting. Together, they embarked on a shared journey, committed to following the Narrow Path and embracing a life of faith.

Stepping out in faith, Sylwia and Brad made a bold decision to open an ice cream parlor, named Sylwia's Ice Cream after Sylwia herself.

Their endeavor was marked by divine favor as their ice cream quickly became renowned and beloved. They garnered numerous awards and accolades, featured on television shows, in newspapers, and magazines.

Notably, they achieved the prestigious "Best of Gulf Shore" award in 2021, were finalists in 2022, and once again claimed victory in 2023.

Sylwia's journey is one of courage, faith, and the pursuit of dreams. From her humble beginnings in Poland to her thriving business and spiritual awakening, she embodies the resilience and unwavering spirit of a woman who trusts in God's guiding hand. Her story is an inspiration to all who long to embrace their dreams and nurture a deep and personal relationship with the Divine.

Introduction

Why I Wrote "Letters of Love"

In our fast-paced world, where instant messages and emails have become the norm, the art of expressing love through heartfelt letters is slowly fading away. We often forget the beauty of taking a moment to pen down our deepest feelings, thoughts, and affections. It is in this context that I was inspired to write "Letters of Love," a book that celebrates the power and significance of personal, handwritten letters filled with love and affection.

In today's rush, it is easy to overlook the enchanting allure of a love letter. Yet, it is through these letters that we have the opportunity to pause, reflect, and express our love to our partners in a profound and intimate way.

I encourage everyone to embrace the act of writing personal letters, as they hold a special place in the recipient's heart and evoke a sense of excitement and anticipation.

While technology offers various ways to communicate, I believe there is a unique charm in the tangible and tactile nature of a handwritten letter.

However, I am also fully aware that the younger generation may prefer typing their letters, and that is perfectly acceptable. The key lies in the act of intentionally crafting a letter and sending it through the mail, regardless of the medium.

"Letters of Love," is not just about the celebration of romantic love; it is a call to express love in all its forms. It is a reminder that love should not be confined to specific occasions such as anniversaries, birthdays, or Valentine's Day.

Instead, we should seize every opportunity to convey our love to the person who holds a special place in our lives, simply because they deserve to feel cherished and valued.

The purpose of this book is to encourage and inspire others to express their love in a letter, rather than through a text or email. It is a gentle reminder to pause and reflect on the beautiful connection we share with our partners, and not to take their presence for granted.

Each letter in this collection is crafted with care and thoughtfulness, aiming to help individuals articulate their emotions, and convey their deepest affections in a meaningful way.

Furthermore, at the core of "Letters of Love" is the foundation of our faith in Jesus Christ. My husband, Brad, has been a significant inspiration for this book. His exceptional qualities - a golden heart, a brilliant mind, and a love for Jesus that shines in his every action.

Our journey of love, faith, and companionship has been a beautiful testament to the power of love that is rooted in mutual respect and shared beliefs.

It is our story, and the stories of many like us that I wish to celebrate and share through this book.

As Christians, we strive to emulate the love that Jesus exemplified during His time on Earth. His love was deep, selfless, and unwavering. It is this divine love that we aim to express in our relationships and marriages.

In "Letters of Love," you will find Christian love letters that intertwine the beauty of faith with the depth of love, showing how the two can intertwine, and flourish.

My hope is that as you journey through the pages of this book, you will be inspired to pick up a pen and write a letter to someone you hold dear.

In a world that often rushes past, take a moment to slow down, to express, and to love. Let the art of letter writing rekindle the flame of love in your relationships, and let your words create lasting memories and deepen the bonds that hold you together.

May "Letters of Love" be a gentle reminder that love is meant to be expressed, celebrated, and cherished. May it inspire you to embark on your own letter-writing journey and bring forth the joy and beauty that comes from the heartfelt expression of love.

With love and blessings,
Sylwia Mills

Chapter 1: First Blooms - The Awakening of Love

Introduction

In the garden of our hearts, love often blooms unexpectedly. It arrives quietly, casting a delicate yet enchanting spell, and before we know it, we're captivated. This first chapter, "First Blooms - The Awakening of Love," explores these initial moments of enchantment.

The beginning stages of love can be wonderfully overwhelming. It's a flurry of nervous excitement, longing glances, and heartbeats that quicken at the mere thought of the other person. It's about the joy of discovering one another, the thrill of each shared moment, and the hope of what might become. It's a time when every conversation, every encounter, sparks a myriad of emotions that make us feel alive in a way we've never felt before.

In this chapter, you'll find a collection of ten letters, each capturing different facets of these early stages of love. From the stirring of new feelings to the joy of connection, these letters offer a glimpse into the magic of new love and its power to transform us. As you read these letters, allow yourself to reminisce about your own experiences of first love or to dream about the love that might be just around the corner. Let these letters remind you of the beauty of vulnerability and the courage it takes to open your heart to another.

Whether you're in the throes of new love or simply wishing to revisit those initial moments of fascination and wonder, I hope these letters inspire you and resonate with your experiences.

Chapter 1: First Blooms - The Awakening of Love

Letter 1: "Stirring of the Heart"
Letter 2: "Igniting the Flame"
Letter 3: "The Spark of Connection"
Letter 4: "Magic in the Air"
Letter 5: "The Nonverbal Communicator"

Chapter 1: Letter 1: Stirring of the Heart

Dear [Her Name],

I'm writing this letter because I want to share something with you. It's a little bit strange and wonderful, and it's all about a feeling that's been growing in me since we met just a few days ago.

I've noticed that I'm smiling more, laughing more, and feeling more energized. My heart feels lighter and there's a certain happiness that lingers even after our conversations end. I find myself thinking about you, about your infectious laughter, the spark in your eyes, and the dreams you've shared. You've brought an excitement and calm into my world that is hard to describe.

In the quiet moments, I replay our conversations and find myself looking forward to the next time we talk. It's a strange feeling, like an adventure that's just starting. It's exciting because it's new and unknown, and a little scary because my heart is starting to hope for more.

Writing this letter is my way of sharing these feelings with you. I want to be honest about what I'm feeling, and about how much I admire you. I also want to learn more about you. But, I'm a little nervous too. I'm not sure what you'll think or feel after reading this. Will you feel the same? Will this make us closer or push us apart?

But even with all the uncertainty, I felt like I had to write this. Because these feelings, these stirrings in my heart, want to be expressed. They want to be shared with you.

So, here it is. My feelings, my admiration, my hope, all here in this letter. It's a small step, an attempt to express the start of something that I hope will grow into something beautiful.

With all respect and warmth,
[Your Name]

Chapter 1: Letter 2: Igniting the Flame

Dear [Her Name],

It's been a while since we met, and I've been feeling something stirring inside me that I can no longer keep to myself. Our interactions, our shared laughter, and the moments our eyes meet - they all seem to ignite a flame within my heart that glows brighter each day.

Your words, your laughter, and your thoughts - they all act as fuel, sparking an excitement in me that I've never quite experienced before. It's both exhilarating and comforting, like a flame that warms yet thrills.

Each time we interact, I find myself looking forward to the next. Your wit, your kindness, and your passion captivate me. Your presence brings a warmth I can't resist, drawing me in like a moth to a flame.

This feeling, this flame, is potent and intense. It can be a little frightening, wondering what might happen if the flame grows too big, too fierce. But despite these fears, the excitement of this journey we're embarking on together overshadows any apprehension.

As we continue to learn more about each other, my hope is that we can nurture this connection, this warmth, and this burgeoning flame.

As I pen this letter, please know that you've already lit a flame in my heart that yearns to grow. The potential of

what we might become is thrilling to me, and I eagerly await our next interaction.
With warmth and anticipation,
[Your Name]

Chapter 1: Letter 3: The Spark of Connection

Hey [Her Name],

So, I've been thinking. Yeah, I know, dangerous pastime, right? But hear me out. Ever since we met, I've noticed this kind of… spark. It's not like fireworks or anything (well, maybe a little bit), but more like that awesome feeling when you finally get the last piece of a puzzle to fit. It just feels right, you know?

Our conversations are like the best kind of movie marathons – unpredictable, engaging, and full of laughter. And that's the thing - I can't remember the last time I laughed as much as I do when we're talking. You've got this way of seeing the funny side of life that's seriously contagious.

Every time we hang out, it's like flipping the channel to my favorite show - it's comfortable, it's fun, and I never want it to end. And the more we talk, the more I feel like I'm getting to know you, and the more I like what I see.

Now, don't get me wrong, I'm not saying we're like two peas in a pod or anything. We're different enough to keep things interesting, but there's this vibe, a connection. It's like we're reading from the same book, even if we're not always on the same page.

Look, I'm not great with words, and I'm pretty sure this letter is proof of that, but I just had to let you know

what's been going on in my mind. I've felt this spark between us, and I'm excited to see where it could lead.
I don't know what you think about all this, but I'd love to hear your thoughts. In the meantime, I'll be here, probably still laughing at that joke you told yesterday.

Catch you later,
[Your Name]

Chapter 1: Letter 4: Magic in the Air

Hey [Her Name],

So, you know that moment when you step outside, and it's the perfect temperature, and there's a light breeze, and everything just feels...right? That's kind of what it's been like getting to know you. There's this magic in the air when we're together, and I can't help but feel like something special is happening.

Our conversations are like a breath of fresh air. You've got this knack for making the ordinary sound extraordinary. Like that time you were talking about your weekend trip to the grocery store and turned it into an epic saga. I mean, who knew the produce aisle could be so exciting?

And the way you laugh, it's like music. It's the kind of sound that makes everything else just fade into the background. It's infectious, and it always leaves me wanting to find new ways to hear it again.

Getting to know you has been like discovering a new favorite song. At first, it's all new and exciting, and then, before you know it, you're humming along, and it feels like you've known it forever.

What I'm trying to say is, there's a kind of magic when we're together. I don't know how else to describe it. It's like we're on the same wavelength, and everything just clicks. I

find myself looking forward to our next conversation, our next laugh, and our next shared moment.
I don't know if you feel it too, this magic in the air, but I thought I'd take a shot and put it out there. Either way, I'm looking forward to more of our conversations, more of your laughter, and more of this magic we've stumbled upon.

Till our next chat,
[Your Name]

Chapter 1: Letter 5: The Nonverbal Communicator

Hey [Her Name],

I wanted to share something with you, and it's a bit different. It's about the things that aren't said out loud but the things that are felt more than they are spoken.

There are times, when I catch myself watching you when you're not looking. Not in a creepy way, I promise! It's more about those moments when you're just being yourself. When you're caught up in a book, or when you're gazing out the window, lost in thought. There's something about those quiet, unguarded moments that speaks volumes.

It's in the way you brush your hair back when you're focused, or the small smile that plays on your lips when you're reading something you enjoy. It's in the way your eyes light up when you talk about something you're passionate about. These small, subtle things - they're like a silent language that only I've been privileged to understand.

And you know what? I've started to write a little poem about it:

Your silence speaks, it whispers soft, In
quiet moments, when thoughts aloft.
A look, a smile, a gentle touch,

Says more than words could ever
clutch. In your gaze, a world unfolds, A
story waiting to be told.
In every look and every sigh,
A universe in your eye.

Isn't it strange how much can be said without uttering a single word? These nonverbal cues, these quiet moments - they're like a secret language, and I feel lucky to be learning it.

I just wanted you to know that I see you - all of you - and I appreciate these silent moments just as much as our lively chats.

Looking forward to more silent and spoken moments,
[Your Name]

Chapter 1: Letter 6: The Dance of Hearts

Dearest [Her Name],

I find myself seated here, once again, poised at the edge of a page, ready to dance with words in an effort to express the intricate waltz my heart seems to be performing lately. As music notes flow from a violin, bringing forth an ethereal melody, so too, I hope my words might flow, bearing the tune of my heart.

This dance, it's a peculiar one. It's as though our hearts have found a rhythm of their own, beating in a tandem that is both new and incredibly enchanting. I find that my heart now beats not solely to the rhythm of my own life, but also to the rhythm of yours.

I imagine our hearts, these brave little drummers, stepping onto the dance floor of emotions. Tentative at first, then growing bolder, moving to the music of our growing connection. A dance that's as old as time, yet fresh as the morning dew.

There's a quiet joy in this synchronization, a harmony that sings of companionship and shared dreams. It's as though our hearts are learning a new language together, a language of care, understanding, and potential affection.

This dance isn't always graceful. There are missteps and awkward pauses, times when the rhythm falters, and our hearts stumble. But that's part of the dance, isn't it? It's in these moments that the dance becomes truly ours, unique in its imperfections.

As we continue to explore this dance, I look forward to the music we will create together, the rhythms we will discover, and the silent language our hearts will learn to speak. It's a dance I am honored to be part of, and one I hope will continue for many more beats of our hearts.

With anticipation of our next waltz,
[Your Name]

Chapter 1: Letter 7: An Uncharted Journey

Dear [Her Name],

As I write this letter, I can't help but feel a sense of adventure. Our journey, this path we're just beginning to explore, is uncharted. It's new and filled with so many unknowns. But I find myself not daunted, but rather excited by the possibilities. Excited by the idea of uncovering the layers of our connection, like an explorer discovering new landscapes.

You see, my heart is in a place of genuine admiration for you. It's in a place of respect for your kindness, your spirit, and the unique person that you are. It's in a place where it can see the beauty in your soul, and it's captivated.

As we navigate this uncharted journey, I want you to know that I'm here, ready to listen, ready to understand, and ready to grow with you. I'm here to celebrate your triumphs, offer a shoulder during times of distress, and to encourage you as we encounter the unforeseen.

I want to know your dreams, your fears, your joys, and your sorrows. I want to understand what makes you laugh, what makes you feel alive, what stirs your heart, and fuels your passion. I yearn to understand the story behind your smile, the hope in your eyes, and the strength in your spirit.

In this journey, I'm not looking for perfection. I'm looking for authenticity, for a connection that goes beyond the surface. I'm looking for shared moments of honesty, of vulnerability, of love, and of growth.
While I know that every journey has its own share of hills and valleys, I also know that it's these experiences that make the journey memorable. And so, I find myself eager to embark on this journey with you, to create our own map filled with shared experiences and heartfelt moments.

My dear [Her Name], I want you to know that my affection for you is real. It's honest and it's growing with each passing day. As we embark on this uncharted journey, I hope you know that my heart is open, ready to embrace all the possibilities that lie ahead.

Looking forward to our next adventure,
[Your Name]

Chapter 1: Letter 8: The Heart's Expedition

Dear [Her Name],

Every journey begins with a single step, they say, and I feel like my heart has embarked on an extraordinary journey. A journey that began the moment I met you. It's an expedition into the uncharted territories of affection, where every turn unveils new landscapes of feelings and emotions.

Each conversation with you feels like an exciting new discovery, like coming across a hidden waterfall in a dense forest or finding a rare gem in a deep mine. Your thoughts, your dreams, your laughter – they're the landmarks on this expedition, guiding me through the wilderness of this newfound love.

The more I get to know you, the deeper I venture into this journey. It's like climbing a mountain, each step bringing a new perspective, a new understanding of you, and of the feelings that you awaken in me. The higher I climb, the more beautiful the view gets, and the stronger my resolve to reach the summit. You are that summit, the peak of this emotional journey, and I can't wait to reach it.

But an expedition isn't about the destination alone. It's about the journey, the challenges faced, the lessons learned, and the memories made. So, I don't want to rush this journey. I want to enjoy each moment, each conversation, each laughter, and even each silence. I want to cherish the process of knowing you, of understanding you, and of falling for you. Because that's where the real magic lies.

So, here's to our journey, to our expedition of the heart. May it be filled with discoveries, joy, and a love that grows with each passing day.

With all my affection,
[Your Name]

Chapter 1: Letter 9: Symphony of Emotions

Dear [Her Name],

I hope this letter finds you well. I sit down to write to you again, this time with a whirlwind of emotions twirling inside me, a symphony, if you will, each note hitting a different chord, expressing a different feeling.

I am excited, that's for sure. The thrill of getting to know you, the joy of discovering new aspects of your personality, the pleasure of our conversations - it's all exhilarating. And yet, I find myself feeling a little apprehensive, a little anxious.

The anxiety stems not from you, but from the vulnerability that this journey of love demands. It's the fear of the unknown, the uncertainty of what the future holds, and the apprehension of how our feelings might evolve. It's a strange mix of exhilaration and nervousness, like standing on the edge of a cliff, ready to dive into the unknown.

There are moments when I find myself pondering about what you might be feeling, wondering if you're experiencing the same symphony of emotions. There are times, when I wish I could peer into your thoughts and understand what's going on in your mind. I wonder if you also feel the thrill, the excitement, and the little bit of fear that comes with this beautiful journey that we've embarked on together.

So, I write this letter to you today, laying my feelings bare, hoping that this honesty will open up a channel for us to share more openly. I want to understand you better, to know your fears and your dreams, your joys, and your worries. I want to know where we stand in each other's lives.

This is a leap of faith for me. It's easier for me to express my feelings in writing, to articulate my thoughts with precision and thoughtfulness. I hope that this letter will bring us closer, that it will help us navigate the symphony of emotions that this journey of love brings with it.

It's okay if you're not ready to open up completely. We're all a work in progress, and it's okay to take our time. All I ask is for honesty and open communication.

Here's to the symphony of emotions, to the beautiful music that our hearts are creating. I look forward to hearing from you, to understanding your melody, and harmonizing our notes together.

With warmth and sincerity,
[Your Name]

Chapter 1: Letter 10: The Art of Falling in Love

Dear [Her Name],

Have you ever watched a painter at work? Carefully, they select their colors, choosing the perfect brush, and then with a deep breath, they make that first stroke on the canvas. From there, it's a dance of color and emotion, each stroke a testament to their vision and creativity, until finally, a masterpiece is born.

Falling in love, I think, is a lot like that. It's an art in itself, a beautiful dance of emotions and experiences, each moment adding a new color to the canvas of our relationship. And just like art, there is no set pattern or rulebook to follow. Each story of love is unique, a masterpiece in its own right.

Since our paths crossed, I've found myself deep in this artistry, experiencing feelings and emotions that are as exhilarating as they are terrifying. There's the rush of joy when we talk, the comfort in your laughter, and the anticipation of our next conversation. There's also the worry of misunderstanding, the fear of not being enough, and the hope for something beautiful.

Each of these feelings, as different as they are, come together to create a beautiful mix, like different hues on a painter's palette. They add depth and dimension to the canvas of our growing relationship, making it all the more beautiful.

And amidst all this, I've realized something. Falling in love is not just about the grand gestures or the romantic moments. It's in the small things too. It's in the way you light up when you talk about something you love. It's in your kindness and your compassion. It's in the way your presence brings a sense of calm and happiness.

This journey, this process of falling in love, is an art. And I am here, ready with my palette of emotions, ready to create this masterpiece with you. The canvas is still largely blank, and there's so much more to add, so much more to experience. But I'm excited about the possibilities, about the beautiful artwork that we could create together.

I don't know what the final picture will look like. Maybe it will be a beautiful landscape filled with sunshine and laughter, or maybe a starry night filled with deep conversations and shared dreams. Whatever it is, I know it will be beautiful, because it will be a reflection of us, of our journey, and of our love.

And so, I eagerly pick up my brush, ready for the next stroke on our canvas. Here's to the art of falling in love, to the beautiful masterpiece we are creating.

With warmth and admiration,
[Your Name]

Chapter 2: "Deepening Bonds - The Growth of Love"

Introduction

This chapter delves into the profound journey of love as it evolves and deepens between two individuals. It is a chapter that celebrates the transformative power of love, highlighting how it has the ability to strengthen connections and bring about beautiful growth within a relationship.

In this chapter, we embark on an exploration of the various facets of love's growth. We witness the unfolding of love's potential, as two hearts intertwine and discover new depths of understanding and intimacy. It is a time of profound connection, where the bonds between two individuals deepen and strengthen.

Throughout the letters in this chapter, we encounter the resilience that love brings, as it weathers challenges and overcomes obstacles. It is a testament to the power of love to transcend the mundane and transform lives. We witness the growth and transformation that love can inspire, as it leads individuals on a journey of self-discovery and mutual understanding.

The letters in this chapter serve as windows into the ever evolving nature of love. They portray the profound beauty that emerges when two individuals commit to

nurturing their connection, fostering growth, and allowing their love to flourish.
As we immerse ourselves in this chapter, we are invited to reflect on our own experiences of love and the ways in which it has deepened and evolved. We are reminded of the transformative power of love, the joy of discovery, and the unbreakable bonds that form when two souls are united in their pursuit of a shared future.

Through the letters in Chapter 2, we are encouraged to embrace the growth that love offers and to nurture the connections that have the potential to enrich our lives. It is a chapter that celebrates the beautiful journey of love, reminding us that as we invest in our relationships, and open ourselves to vulnerability, we pave the way for love to flourish and for our hearts to be forever changed.

Chapter 2: Deepening Bonds - The Growth of Love

Chapter 2: Letter 1: Roots Entwining

Dear [Her Name],

The more I come to know you, the more I find myself intertwining with you, much like the roots of two trees growing together in a dense forest. Our conversations, shared laughs, and moments of quiet understanding seem to weave together, creating a connection that grows stronger with each passing day.

I've noticed that the rhythm of my day begins to align with yours. The anticipation of our interactions adds a certain excitement to my daily routine. And even when we are not together, I find myself reflecting on our shared experiences and looking forward to the next.

I'm beginning to understand that this is more than a simple friendship. Our connection has started to deepen, to grow roots. It's like we are learning a new language together, one made up of shared experiences, inside jokes, and silent understandings. This connection feels organic, natural like it was always meant to be.

What I find truly fascinating is how our lives, which were once parallel, are now starting to intersect. Our interests, our dreams, and even our challenges, seem to be aligning in ways I could not have predicted. It's as if God is gently nudging us toward each other, showing us how well we fit together.

But what I appreciate most is the sense of comfort and familiarity that comes with our growing connection. It's the comfort of knowing that there is someone who understands my thoughts before I voice them, someone who can make me laugh even on my worst days, and someone who sees the world through a lens similar to mine.

I don't know where this journey will lead us, [Her Name], but I'm excited to find out. I'm excited to continue growing with you, to continue intertwining our lives, and to see where this path of shared experiences takes us.

For now, I just wanted to express my appreciation for you and for the connection that we've started to cultivate. I look forward to seeing where our intertwined roots will grow.

With warm regards,
[Your Name]

Chapter 2: Letter 2: The Deepening River – The Flow of Our Love

Dear [Her Name],

Over the course of our relationship, I've noticed that our connection is much like a river. It's constantly moving, constantly changing, but always flowing. It's filled with moments of calm, but also moments of rapid intensity that take our breath away.

And just like a river, our love seems to have a direction. It's pushing us towards something greater, something beyond ourselves. It's an exciting, sometimes challenging journey, but one that I'm grateful to be on with you.

It's in the quiet moments that I feel this the most. When we're together, sharing a simple conversation, I find myself swept up in the current of our connection. It's as if God himself is guiding us, helping us to navigate the waters of our relationship.

But it's not just the big moments that make our relationship special. It's also the small, seemingly insignificant ones. The brief texts during the day, the shared smiles, the quiet understanding... these are the drops that make up our river of love.

I write this letter to express my admiration for the way we have continued to flow together, navigating the twists and turns of life as a unified stream. I am continually amazed at how our love deepens, how our connection

strengthens, and how our journey together continues to unfold.
As we continue to navigate this river of love, I hope that we will face the rapids with courage, enjoy the calm stretches with gratitude, and always keep our eyes on the horizon, excited for the journey ahead.

With all my affection,
[Your Name]

Chapter 2: Letter 3: The Blossoming Tree – Our Relationship in Full Bloom

Dear [Her Name],

It's as if our relationship is a tree that has been planted, tenderly cared for and is now blossoming in full bloom. Each day that passes, each moment we share is like a ray of sunshine, a drop of rain, nurturing our love, and helping it to grow.

Remember when we planted the seed of this love? It was a simple connection, a shared smile, a moment that sparked something within both of us. From that moment, our love began to grow. It was small at first, just like a sapling. But with each passing day, each passing moment, it began to grow stronger, taller, and more resilient.

And now, here we are, standing in the shadow of this magnificent tree of love that we've grown together. Its branches are wide, providing shelter from life's storms. Its roots run deep, a testament to the strength of our bond. And its leaves are vibrant, reflecting the beauty of our love.

This tree, our relationship, is in full bloom. Each blossom is a beautiful moment, a cherished memory, a milestone in our journey together. And the fragrance of these blooms is intoxicating, filling my senses with the sweet scent of our love.

I look forward to the seasons of growth ahead of us, to the fruit that this tree will bear. I look forward to nurturing this tree, our relationship, with you. Because just like a tree, I believe that our love will continue to grow, continue to blossom, and continue to bear fruit.

With all my love,
[Your Name]

Chapter 2: Letter 4: The Rising Sun – The Brightening of Our Bond

Dear [Her Name],

I hope this letter finds you bathed in the glorious light of a new day, much like the radiant glow that our growing bond is casting on my life. Just like the sun, our connection is becoming brighter, more potent, and more integral to my existence. It is a beacon that guides me, a warmth that comforts me, and a light that illuminates my path.

In this journey of deepening our bond, I've discovered so much about you, and in turn, about myself. Your kindness, your strength, your spirit - each new facet I discover adds another ray of light to the brightening sun that is our relationship. Your love has painted my world in vibrant hues, and each day with you feels like a sunrise that never ends.

Our conversations, our shared laughter, the silent moments we've spent just feeling each other's presence – these are the golden threads that weave the tapestry of our bond. Each day, as the sun rises, it's these threads that shine the brightest, reminding me of the bond we share, and how it is growing stronger and more radiant with each passing moment.

It's humbling and awe-inspiring to think about how our bond has brightened and deepened, just like the rising sun. It's been a beautiful and enriching journey, one that I hope continues for many more sunrises.

I'm writing this letter to celebrate the brightening of our bond, to appreciate the light it's brought into my life, and to express how much I'm looking forward to witnessing many more sunrises with you. Like a sunflower turning to the sun, my heart yearns for the light of your love, and I am excited to see how our relationship continues to grow and brighten.

May the Lord continue to guide us on this path, and may our bond continue to brighten just like the rising sun.

With all my affection,
[Your Name]

Chapter 2: Letter 5: Harvest Moon – Reaping the Love We Have Sown

Dear [Her Name],

As I pen down this letter under the enchanting gaze of the harvest moon, I am filled with an overwhelming sense of gratitude and wonderment. The harvest moon, in its quiet magnificence, is a symbol of abundance and the fruition of hard work. In its light, I see a reflection of our love – the love we have nurtured, cultivated, and now are reaping.

Our bond, much like the harvest moon, has grown from a tiny speck of light in the vast canvas of the night sky to a beacon of love that shines brightly, illuminating our paths. Every conversation, every shared silence, every laugh, every tear, and every moment we have spent together has been a seed sown in the soil of our love. And now, my love, we are standing in the midst of a bountiful harvest, reaping the love that we have so diligently sown and nurtured.

Much like the farmers who patiently tend to their fields, we too have labored over our bond. We have watered it with kindness, pruned it with understanding, and shielded it from the harsh winds of doubt and fear. And just as the harvest moon signals the time to reap what has been sown, I feel it's time for us to celebrate the love that has blossomed from our joint efforts.

Our journey together hasn't always been easy, but it has always been worth it. We have navigated through the seasons of our love, and now under this harvest moon, I feel a sense of completion, a sense of contentment, as if we have reached a milestone in our journey. But I know that this is not the end, it is just another beautiful chapter in our ever-evolving love story.

As we continue this journey under God's watchful eyes, let's remember to always nurture our bond, to patiently tend to it, and to never stop sowing seeds of love. For I know that as long as we are together, every harvest will be bountiful, every moon will be a harvest moon, and every letter that I write will be a testament to the incredible love we share.

Here's to us, to our love, and to many more harvest moons together.

Yours lovingly,
[Your Name]

Chapter 2: Letter 6: Mountain Peaks – The Heights Our Love Can Reach

Dear [Her Name],

You know, I've always been fascinated by mountains. Their sheer majesty, their unyielding resilience, and their quiet but profound wisdom. They stand tall against the harshest of storms, and yet they remain humble enough to let the rivers flow freely down their slopes. They reach for the heavens, yet remain firmly rooted in the earth.

Our love, my dear, reminds me of these magnificent mountains. It is strong and enduring, yet it flows with a gentle grace that soothes my soul. It dreams of reaching the heights of the heavens, yet it remains grounded in the realities of life.

With every passing day, I feel our love is growing stronger, reaching higher, much like a mountain peak piercing the clouds. We have weathered storms and braved winds together, and with each challenge, our bond has only solidified, much like the mountain that stands tall against the harshest of weather.

But my love, the most beautiful aspect of a mountain is not its peak. It is the journey to the top. The winding trails, the breathtaking views, the shared laughter, and moments of quiet reflection, they are what makes the climb worthwhile. And our journey of love, with all its ups and downs, twists and turns, moments of joy, and moments of challenge is what makes our love so beautiful, so real.

As we continue this journey together, know that I am here, by your side, ready to climb every mountain, traverse every trail, and reach every peak with you. For I am certain that no matter how high the peak, our love can reach it. And no matter how challenging the climb, our bond can withstand it. For our love is like the mountain - strong, enduring, and ever-reaching toward the heavens.

With all my love,
[Your Name]

Chapter 2: Letter 7: The Guiding Stars – Navigating Our Love's Journey

Dear [Her Name],

On clear nights, when the sky is a canvas of celestial wonder, I often find myself gazing at the stars. They are constant and unchanging, each one a beacon in the night, guiding travelers on their journey. It reminds me of our love - a guiding star, a constant light in my life.

With every twinkle, every shimmer, they seem to whisper a silent promise, much like the one our hearts made when they met. The stars have their constellations, and we, with our shared moments and memories, each one a shining point on the map of our journey.

I can't tell you how many times I've looked up at the night sky, only to feel the pull of our connection. It's as if our souls are tethered, always pulling us back to each other, no matter how far we may drift apart. It's a comforting thought, knowing that there's this unseen force that always leads me back to you, to our love.

Navigating through life with you feels like following the North Star. Even in the darkest times, your love shines bright, guiding me through uncertainty, and showing me the way when I'm lost. Our love is the compass that always points me home, and for that, I am eternally grateful.

I look forward to navigating the rest of our journey together, guided by our love, our shared dreams, and the promise of many more beautiful moments to come. I know there will be challenges, but I am confident that our love, our guiding star, will see us through.

With all my love,
[Your Name]

Chapter 2: Letter 8: The Ocean's Depths – Exploring Our Deepening Feelings

Dear [Her Name],

There are moments when I feel our love is akin to the ocean. It holds such depth and vastness that I find myself continually enchanted, forever desiring to explore its depths. You, my love, are the sea that holds a world teeming with emotions, a world that I'm blessed to plunge into, discover, and understand more with each passing day.

Yet, as we dive deeper, I also find myself feeling vulnerable. Just like a diver venturing into the ocean, I'm stepping into territories unknown, experiencing feelings I have not felt before. There are currents of emotions, like waves that could be strong and overwhelming. It can be frightening, and yet I wouldn't want it any other way. I want to navigate this ocean with you, even through all the waves and the tides, because it is with you that I want to share all of my deepest feelings and thoughts.

It is through this journey that I have come to appreciate the beauty of vulnerability. To let you see my heart, in all its truth, is like revealing the secret treasures hidden deep within the ocean. It is both liberating and frightening, but it is the most genuine expression of my love for you. I hope that as I unveil my heart, you too feel safe and comfortable enough to reveal your depths to me.

As we continue to deepen our bond, I want you to know that I am here, committed to understanding, and loving you, just as you are. I am here, ready to brave the waves, dive into the depths, and explore the vast expanse of our love.

Yours in deep affection,
[Your Name]

Chapter 2: Letter 9: The Growing Garden – Nurturing Our Shared Dreams

Dear [Her Name],

I hope this letter finds you well, invigorated by the thought of a new day, as I am by the thought of you. Our love is like a garden, a place where dreams are planted, where they take root in the rich soil of shared emotions, hopes, and aspirations. It's a place of growth, of change, and above all, of nurturing.

You know, when I was a kid, I used to help my mom in the garden. I remember how she'd plant seeds in the ground with such care and tenderness, and then she'd water them, watch over them, and wait. It was a labor of love, I see now. She showed me that a garden is not just a patch of earth, but a living testament to patience, dedication, and hope.

That's how I see our love. It's not just a feeling, but a commitment to nurture the seeds of our dreams, to water them with understanding, to watch over them with patience, and to wait for them to bloom with the changing seasons of our life together.

We have sown the seeds of our dreams in the fertile ground of our love. Each day, we water them with laughter and shared moments, we let the sunshine of our affection warm them, and we protect them from the harsh winds of misunderstandings with our unwavering communication. And just as a gardener waits for the first sprouts to break through the soil, we wait for our dreams to take shape and grow.

As we move forward in our journey, let's continue to nurture our shared dreams. Let's give them all the love and care they need to flourish, just like we do for each other.
Let's watch them grow, together, in our garden of love.

Forever yours,
[Your Name]

Chapter 2: Letter 10: The Warming Heart – Our Love's Comforting Embrace

Dear [Her Name],

You know when you come home after a long day, and you just sink into a comfy chair, kick off your shoes, and relax? That's what our love feels like to me. It's the warm, comforting embrace that wraps around me at the end of the day. It's the glowing hearth that I return to, again and again, drawing me in with its familiar warmth and comforting light.

Our love is the safe haven that shields us from the world's storms. It's the sanctuary where we can be our true selves, where we can share our deepest thoughts and dreams without fear of judgment. It's the cozy den where we snuggle up together, whispering sweet nothings, laughing at shared jokes, and basking in the glow of our shared affection.

The fire in our hearth burns brightly, fueled by our shared dreams and ambitions, our mutual respect and understanding, and the deep, abiding love we have for each other. Even on the coldest nights, it keeps us warm. Even in the darkest times, it lights our way. And like a beacon, it guides us home, back to each other's arms, where we belong.

As we deepen our bond, let's keep the hearth of our love burning brightly. Let's feed it with our shared experiences, our dreams, and our love. Let's stoke its flames with our passion, our commitment, and our mutual respect. And let's bask in its warm glow, comforted by the knowledge that no matter where we go, we always have a home in each other's hearts.

All my love,
[Your Name]

Chapter 3: Challenges - The Test of Love

Introduction

This chapter delves into the complexities and trials that love faces as it encounters various challenges. It explores the strength, resilience, and depth of love when put to the test. In this chapter, we witness the ways in which love can overcome obstacles, navigate through difficulties, and grow even stronger amidst adversity.

The 10 letters in this chapter encapsulate different aspects of love's journey through challenges. Each letter offers a unique perspective on the trials and tribulations that couples may encounter in their relationship. From weathering storms to overcoming differences, from rebuilding connections to finding one's way through complexities, these letters reflect the real-life challenges that love often confronts.

Through vulnerability, honesty, forgiveness, and a steadfast commitment to one another, the couples in these letters demonstrate the power of love to overcome obstacles and emerge stronger on the other side. This chapter serves as a reminder that love is not without its tests, but it is in facing and conquering these challenges that love deepens and grows.

In the following letters, you will witness the couples' journey through the challenges they face, their unwavering faith in love, and their commitment to overcoming the tests that come their way. Each letter provides insight into the transformative power of love when confronted with obstacles, as well as the enduring strength of love in the face of adversity.

Chapter 3: Challenges - The Test of Love

Letter 1: "Stormy Weather - Weathering Love's Trials"
Letter 2: "Mountain Pass - Overcoming Obstacles Together"
Letter 3: "The Rough Seas - Navigating Love's Challenges"
Letter 4: "The Untraveled Road - Venturing into the Unknown"

Letter 5: "The Love Knot - Untangling Our Differences" Letter 6: "Nights of Darkness - Finding Each Other in the Shadows"
Letter 7: "The Winding Path - Walking through Complexities"
Letter 8: "The Broken Bridge - Rebuilding Our Connection"
Letter 9: "Love's Labyrinth - Finding Our Way Through"
Letter 10: "The Steep Climb - Scaling Love's Challenges"

Chapter 3: Letter 1: Stormy Weather – Weathering Love's Trials

My Beloved,

In the symphony of our shared existence, the notes have not always been harmonious. We have weathered storms together, storms that have tested our unity, our resolve, and our faith in one another. But it is said that trials teach us who we are, they dig up the soil and let us see what we are made of. And through every storm, we have uncovered not only our individual strengths but the power of our bond.

It is in these moments of hardship that I find myself reflecting on the nature of our love. I see us, not as two beings caught in a storm, but as two halves of a whole weathering the trials together. This, in itself, is a testament to the depth of our love. For trials are medicines that our gracious and wise God prescribes because we need them; He proportions the frequency and weight of them to what the case requires.

Often, we endure trials seeking God's deliverance from them. Suffering is painful for us to endure or to see those we love endure. While our instinct is to flee trials, remember that even in the midst of suffering, God's will is being done. Like a river that cuts through a mountain not out of spite for the mountain, but simply to reach the sea, these trials are not punishments but pathways.

Through the stormy weather, I have seen us grow. I have seen us endure. I have seen us come out stronger. For we are always in the forge, or on the anvil; by trials God is shaping us for higher things. Our love, like a ship, becomes stronger and more reliable after it has weathered a storm. And so, even as we face these trials, I find comfort in knowing that we are being shaped into better versions of ourselves.

Our love story is not one that shies away from the harsh realities of life. It is a story that embraces them, learns from them, and ultimately, triumphs over them. The trials we face are not just challenges, they are opportunities to strengthen our bond, to deepen our understanding of each other, and to solidify our shared faith.

Let our love be a beacon that guides us through the storm, let it be our haven, our safe harbor. And remember, the man who has gone through trials and testing successfully, will be strong and capable of doing all the will of God. So, too, will our love grow stronger with each storm we weather together.

Remember, my love, we are not simply weathering a storm; we are learning to dance in the rain.

Yours, in faith and love,
[Your Name]

Chapter 3: Letter 2: Mountain Pass - Overcoming Obstacles Together

My Dear,

The journey of life is often compared to climbing a mountain. It's not always an easy climb. The path is filled with jagged rocks and steep ascents that may cause us to stumble. But, just as the mountain climber presses on, we too must continue on our journey.

It is said that the view from the top of a mountain is only appreciated after a tough climb, and this is true for our lives as well. The trials and tribulations we face are much like those steep inclines and slippery slopes. They test our resilience, our faith, and our determination. Yet, remember that in our struggle, we are not alone. We are blessed with the presence of God and the fellowship of others who, like us, are navigating their own mountains.

Romans 8:28 reminds us; "And we know that all things work together for good to them that love God, to them who are the called according to His purpose." This verse is a beacon of hope when our path seems treacherous. It is a promise that God is always working in our lives, turning even our hardships into blessings. The trials we face are not senseless obstacles; they are part of a larger, divine plan that is inherently good and purposeful.

God calls us to climb, to face our mountains, not because He wants to see us struggle, but because He knows that the journey will strengthen us. The struggles we overcome allow us to develop resilience and grow in our faith. They are opportunities for us to demonstrate our love for God and our dedication to His purpose. Each trial is a chance to learn, grow, and ultimately, to be drawn closer to God.

Just as we don't climb a mountain in a single bound, we don't overcome our trials all at once. It's a process, often a slow and challenging one. But every step we take forward, every obstacle we overcome, brings us closer to the top, closer to a deeper understanding of God's purpose for us.

When we pass through the trials, when we overcome the obstacles in our path, we do so together, hand in hand with God and with each other. We share in each other's burdens, offer encouragement when the climb becomes steep, and celebrate together when we reach a new peak. This shared journey strengthens our bonds with one another and with God.

In this journey, remember to pause often, to look back and see how far you've come. Every peak and valley, every struggle and victory, is a testament to God's grace and your own strength.

As we continue to traverse our mountains, let us do so with faith and perseverance, knowing that with God by our side, no obstacle is insurmountable.

Chapter 3: Letter 2: Mountain Pass - Overcoming Obstacles Together (cont.)

Let us embrace the trials, for they are opportunities for growth, and let us never forget that in all things, God works for the good of those who love Him, who have been called according to His purpose.

With every step, every ascent, let us remember Romans 8:28, and know that we are loved, we are guided, and we are never alone on this journey.

With love and blessings,
[Your Name]

Chapter 3: Letter 3: The Rough Seas – Navigating Love's Challenges

My Dearest,

With every day that passes, our journey of love feels more like a voyage at sea. There are calm days, where our love is the tranquil water beneath a clear, sunny sky. But there are also stormy days, where we find ourselves navigating the tempestuous waves of life's challenges together.

It's during these challenging times that we must remember the promise in Romans 8:28, that "we know that in all things God works for the good of those who love him, who have been called according to his purpose." Our love, rooted in our shared faith, is not immune to trials. But it's these trials that test the strength of our bond and the depth of our commitment to each other.

Just as a ship must navigate the rough seas, we too must find our way through the challenges that come our way. We find ourselves sometimes tossed by the waves of miscommunication, sometimes caught in the storms of misunderstanding, and at other times, we are confronted with the strong winds of differing perspectives. These are our rough seas, our moments of testing.

But I have faith in us. I have faith that our love is like a sturdy ship, built to withstand the storms. As James 1:2-3 reminds us, "Consider it pure joy, my brothers and sisters, whenever you face trials of many kinds because you know that the testing of your faith produces perseverance." Every test in our life is an opportunity for growth and strengthening of our love. It is through these challenges that we can become victors, not victims.

In navigating these challenges, let us remember the encouraging words in 2 Corinthians 4:8-9, "We are hard pressed on every side, but not crushed; perplexed, but not in despair; persecuted, but not abandoned; struck down, but not destroyed." Our love, anchored in our shared faith, will weather the storms and emerge stronger.

As we face these rough seas, let us hold onto the truth of Psalm 46:1, "God is our refuge and strength, an ever present help in trouble." It is our shared faith in God that gives us the strength to face the challenges. It is our love for each other, rooted in His love for us that will help us navigate through these trials.

In spite of the challenges we face, my love for you remains unwavering. In the end, I believe that our voyage through these rough seas will only deepen our love and strengthen our bond. As we navigate these challenges together, let us remember to trust in God's plan for us and to love each other unconditionally, as 1 Corinthians 13:7-8 reminds us, "Love always protects, always trusts, always hopes, always perseveres. Love never fails."

Yours in love and faith, [Your Name]

Chapter 3: Letter 4: The Untraveled Road – Venturing into the Unknown

My Dearest [Spouse's Name],

As we venture forth into the untraveled road of our lives together, we may often find ourselves facing a sense of uncertainty, a testament to our vulnerability as we step into the unknown. Yet, in these moments of hesitation and doubt, we are presented with a beautiful opportunity to surrender ourselves to the divine plan that God has laid out for us. Our journey may be fraught with trials and tribulations, but remember, these trials "teach us what we are; they dig up the soil, and let us see what we are made of."

When we find ourselves on unfamiliar paths, let us find solace in the words of the Bible. Isaiah brings us comfort and strength with the verse, "So do not fear, for I am with you; do not be dismayed, for I am your God. I will strengthen you and help you; I will uphold you with my righteous right hand" (Isaiah 41:10). This reassures us that while we may not know the exact contours of the path ahead, we are never alone in our journey.

The Book of Jeremiah further illuminates our path with hope, "For I know the plans I have for you, declares the Lord, plans for welfare and not for evil, to give you a future and a hope" (Jeremiah 29:11). Our path may be untraveled, but it is not unplanned. It has been thoughtfully laid out by the Lord, with each step we take leading us toward a future filled with hope.

In our journey of love, as we navigate through the road less traveled, we often find ourselves pushing our boundaries, venturing out of our comfort zones, and braving the uncertain in pursuit of the extraordinary. As we step into the unknown, let us remember that our shared faith is our compass, guiding us through the darkness toward the light of His love.

Remember, my love, "We are always in the forge, or on the anvil; by trials God is shaping us for higher things." These trials we face together are but stepping stones, shaping us, molding us, and preparing us for the glorious future that God has planned for us.

As we journey together, let us find courage in His promise and strength in His presence. For He is our guide, our sustainer, and our ultimate destination. Together, hand in hand, we will venture forth into the unknown, bound by our love and fortified by our faith.

Yours in love and faith,
[Your Name]

Chapter 3: Letter 5: The Love Knot – Untangling Our Differences

Dear Beloved,

With each heartbeat, my love for you grows, deepening with every passing moment. We are bound together by a love that is powerful and transformative, yet it is the very essence of our humanity that we are different individuals. These differences could be a source of friction, but they can also be the threads that tie us together in a stronger bond, a love knot that is intricate, complex, and beautiful.

When differences arise, I am reminded of a Biblical verse, "And we know that all things work together for good to them that love God, to them who are the called according to his purpose" (Romans 8:28). This tells me that all things, including our differences, can work together for good in our relationship if we approach them with love and understanding.

I vow to listen to you, to hear your thoughts and your feelings, even when they differ from my own. I promise to respect your perspective and to approach our differences not as a battleground but as a chance for us to grow together. Even when I am convinced that I am right and you are wrong, I pledge to remain humble and open to your point of view. There is a wisdom in

humility, a strength that is born from understanding rather than insistence.
"Trials come to prove and improve us", and our differences are trials of sorts. They test our ability to love, understand, and grow together. But remember, my dear that "the man who has an easy way through life, will be spiritually weak, flabby and impoverished. He won't be able to do all that God wants him to do. But the one who has gone through trials and testing successfully, will be strong and capable of doing all the will of God." Our differences, then are not stumbling blocks but stepping stones to a stronger, deeper love.

Like the Holy Spirit that "has been poured out into our hearts" (Romans 5:5), let us pour understanding, compassion, and humility into our hearts for each other. Let us rejoice in our differences, for they make us who we are and add richness to our shared journey. "My soul glorifies the Lord and my spirit rejoices in God my Savior" (Luke 1:46-47), and it is this divine love that I seek to emulate in our relationship.

In the same way that children are taught to "obey your parents in everything, for this pleases the Lord" (Colossians 3:20), let us learn to obey the commandment of love in our relationship. Let us honor each other and our differences, so that we may live long in the land of love that the Lord has given us.

Beloved, I want to understand you, to celebrate you, and to love you, the differences and all. In your differences, I see the beauty of God's creation, the richness of human experience, and the depth of our love. Let us untangle the love knot together, threading our way through understanding and compassion, tying us ever closer in the bond of love.

With all my love,
[Your Name]

Chapter 3: Letter 6: Night's Darkness – Finding Each Other in the Shadows

My Dearest,

As we navigate the seas of life together, there are times when we find ourselves enveloped by night's darkness. These are the moments when uncertainty looms, questions surge, and shadows seem to extend indefinitely. Yet, it is in these very shadows that we find each other, hand in hand, hearts connected, illuminated by the light of our shared faith.

Have we not learned that darkness is not wholly devoid of light, but merely a stage for it to shine brighter? Have we not found that it is in the pitch black of night that stars twinkle most brilliantly, casting their hopeful glimmers across the vast canvas of the universe? Such is the nature of our journey. The shadows may be daunting, but they are not our destiny.

We are reminded of the profound wisdom embedded in Proverbs 3:5-6: "Trust in the Lord with all your heart and lean not on your own understanding; in all your ways submit to him, and he will make your paths straight." Even when our path is shrouded in darkness, we must remember that our Lord is guiding us, leading us toward His light.

Let's remember Job, who, in the face of immense suffering and darkness, confessed, "I despise myself and repent in dust and ashes." (Job 42:6) It's in this very acknowledgment of our vulnerability and imperfection that we find the seeds of renewal and redemption. As 2 Corinthians 5:17 tells us, "If anyone is in Christ, he is a new creation: The old has gone, the new is here!"

And so, we trust in our Lord, the one who promises to wipe away every tear, the one who declares, "there shall be no more death, nor sorrow, nor crying. There shall be no more pain." (Rev 21:4) We trust that even in the heart of night's darkness, He holds our future in the palm of His hands.

Let's embrace the shadows, not as an end, but as a transition - a pathway to dawn. For every night has its end, and every storm its rainbow. In our shared darkness, let's find the strength to look ahead, to glimpse the first signs of dawn breaking on the horizon. Let's hold on to each other, hold on to our faith, and hold on to the promise of the light that is yet to come.

With all my love,
[Your Name]

Chapter 3: Letter 7: The Winding Path – Walking Through Complexities

Dear [Wife's Name],

The break of dawn painted a beautiful canvas of colors across the sky as I rose from our shared slumber, a gentle reminder of the divine artistry that surrounds us. As I quietly slipped out of our bed, a sense of blissful happiness washed over me. Happiness for you, for us, and for the complexities of our shared life that have brought us closer to each other, and to God.

In the silence of the early morning, I found myself in the kitchen, preparing your favorite breakfast. Each slice of bread, each brewed cup of tea, carries within it a token of my love, a fragment of my heart. As I write this letter to you, I imagine you waking up to find this note placed gently on your breakfast tray, a humble testament to my feelings for you.

Our life together has been a journey, filled with shared joys and trials. Yet, every trial we've faced has not been a stumbling block but a stepping stone - a reminder that "Trials teach us what we are; they dig up the soil, and let us see what we are made of". And every time, we've found not weakness, but strength - a strength that comes not from us, but from our faith in God.

There are moments of vulnerability, moments when the world and its complexities seem overwhelming. Yet, in these moments, I am reminded of our shared faith, of the strength that lies in surrendering to God's will. "My grace is sufficient for you, for my power is made perfect in weakness," (2 Corinthians 12:19) says the Lord. These words bring comfort, knowing that in our vulnerability, His strength is made manifest.

Our love, our bond, is rooted in more than just our feelings for each other. It is nurtured by our shared faith in Jesus Christ, strengthened by our trust in God's plan for us. "For I know the plans I have for you, declares the Lord, plans for welfare and not for evil, to give you a future and a hope." (Jeremiah 29:11) It is this faith, this trust in the divine will that guides us through the winding path of our life together.

As your husband and partner in faith, I want you to know that you are my companion in this journey. Together, we are stronger, not merely because of our love for each other, but because of our love for Christ, who strengthens us. Every trial we face is a testament to our faith, every moment of vulnerability is an opportunity for grace.

As I head out to work, leaving you with these words and a warm breakfast, I want you to remember that you are loved, not just by me, but by our Lord. Let's continue to walk this winding path together, holding hands and hearts, walking through the complexities with faith in our hearts, and Christ in our midst.

With all my love,
[Your Name]

Chapter 3: Letter 8: The Broken Bridge – Rebuilding Our Connection

Dear [Wife's Name],

As I sit here, pen in hand, with a heart burdened by the weight of my recent actions, I humbly write this letter to you. These past few weeks have been filled with distance, and I confess that I have been at fault. My heart has been heavy with remorse, realizing how my silence and the silent treatment that I have given you have caused a deep rift in our connection.

Today, as I sought solace in the presence of God, I felt a gentle nudging in my spirit. The Lord is teaching me the importance of looking within, examining my own heart and actions. He is guiding me to mend what has been broken, to rebuild the bridge that connects our souls.

I want you to know that I am truly sorry for the pain I have caused you. The silence I held was not a reflection of my love for you but rather a misguided attempt to protect myself from vulnerability. I realize now that love thrives in vulnerability, in open and honest communication, even when it is difficult. I have learned that silence can cause more harm than the spoken word, leaving wounds that may take time to heal.

In this moment of reflection, I am reminded of the words in Proverbs 15:1, "A gentle answer turns away wrath, but a harsh word stirs up anger" I have allowed the silence to stir up anger, when what we truly need is gentleness and understanding. Today, I extend my hand to you, reaching across the broken bridge that separates us, in hopes of rebuilding our connection.

I understand that trust has been damaged, and rebuilding it will take time. But, dear [Wife's Name], I am hopeful. I am hopeful that we can work together, with God at the center of our hearts and our relationship to heal the wounds and strengthen our bond. Just as a broken bridge can be mended, so too can our connection be restored.

Let us embark on a journey of rediscovery, exploring the depths of our love and commitment to one another. I long for the weekend of our love, where we can set aside distractions and focus on nurturing our connection. May it be a time of laughter, forgiveness, and grace, as we rebuild what has been damaged.

I want you to know that my love for you is unwavering, even in the midst of my shortcomings. I am committed to learning from my mistakes and growing together with you. Together, let us allow the Lord Jesus Christ to guide us, to fill our hearts with hope, and to show us the path to restoration.

Thank you, for your patience, and forgiveness, and for allowing me the opportunity to rebuild what was broken. I am grateful for your love and presence in my life. Let us take this journey of rebuilding our connection hand in hand, trusting in God's grace to lead us to a deeper love.

With all my love and repentance,

[Your Name]

Chapter 3: Letter 9: The Love's Labyrinth – Finding Our Way Through

Dear [Spouse's Name],

As I sit here, contemplating the intricate path our love has taken, I am reminded of the love's labyrinth we find ourselves in. It seems that at times, the way forward is obscured, and we may feel lost in the twists and turns. Yet, in the midst of this labyrinth, I find solace in knowing that with Christ, all things are possible.

In the book of Matthew, we are reminded of the words of Jesus, "With man this is impossible, but with God all things are possible" (Matthew 19:26). These words offer us hope and reassurance that even in the midst of challenges and complexities, we can find our way through.

Our love's labyrinth may be filled with uncertainties, differences, and obstacles, but I firmly believe that our faith in Christ can guide us to the path of understanding, compassion, and unity. As we navigate this labyrinth, let us hold on to the words in Proverbs 3:5-6, "Trust in the Lord with all your heart and lean not on your own understanding; in all your ways submit to him, and he will make your paths straight."

In the labyrinth of our love, we may encounter moments of doubt, confusion, and fear. But I want you to know that I am committed to finding our way through, hand in hand. Together, let us lean on God's guidance, relying on

His infinite wisdom and grace to lead us to the path of reconciliation and growth.

As we journey through this labyrinth, it is essential that we approach each other with open hearts, willing to listen, and understand. Ephesians 4:2 reminds us to "be completely humble and gentle; be patient, bearing with one another in love." Let us extend grace and patience to one another, knowing that we are both imperfect beings striving to grow in love and unity.

In the midst of the labyrinth, let us not lose sight of the love that binds us together. 1 Peter 4:8 reminds us, "Above all, love each other deeply because love covers over a multitude of sins." Our love has the power to overcome any obstacles we may face, and it can lead us to a deeper understanding and appreciation of one another.

As we continue to navigate this labyrinth, I am grateful for your unwavering love, patience, and commitment. Together, with Christ as our guide, let us press on, knowing that He is faithful to lead us out of the maze and into a place of greater love and unity.

In the labyrinth of our love, I am reminded of the words of Helen Keller, "Love is like a beautiful flower which I may not touch, but whose fragrance makes the garden a place of delight just the same." Let our love's fragrance permeate the labyrinth, illuminating the path before us, and filling our hearts with hope and joy.

With deep love and faith,
[Your Name]

Chapter 3: Letter 10: The Steep Climb – Scaling Love's Challenges

Dear [Spouse's Name],

As I sit here and reflect on the journey we have traveled together, I am reminded of the steep climb we have faced in scaling the challenges that have come our way. Our love has been tested, and I want you to know that I deeply regret any pain or hurt I may have caused you along the way.

In the book of James, we are reminded of the importance of humility and seeking forgiveness. James 4:10 says, "Humble yourselves before the Lord, and he will lift you up".

Today, I humbly come before you, acknowledging my shortcomings and the mistakes I have made. I ask for your forgiveness for any times I have fallen short as a husband, and for any hurtful words or actions that have caused you pain.

In the climb of love's challenges, it is crucial that we face them together, hand in hand. Romans 12:16 encourages us to "live in harmony with one another. Do not be proud, but be willing to associate with people of low position. Do not be conceited."

Let us approach our challenges with humility and a willingness to understand each other's perspectives, knowing

that our unity is stronger than any obstacle that we may encounter.
As we face the steep climb before us, let us not lose sight of the hope that lies ahead. Psalm 31:24 reminds us, "Be strong and take heart, all you who hope in the Lord."

Our hope is not in our own strength but in the Lord, who is faithful to guide us and provide us with the strength we need to overcome any challenges that come our way.

I want you to know that I am committed to facing these challenges head-on, with boldness and determination. Proverbs 28:1 encourages us, "The wicked flee though no one pursues but the righteous are as bold as a lion".

Together, let us be bold in our pursuit of love, trusting in God's grace, and wisdom to guide us.

In the climb of love's challenges, I am reminded of the words of Martin Luther King Jr., "The ultimate measure of a man is not where he stands in moments of comfort and convenience, but where he stands at times of challenge and controversy." Let our love be measured not only by the easy moments but by our unwavering commitment and resilience in the face of challenges.

As we continue this journey together, I want you to know that I am here for you, ready to face any challenge that comes our way. With God's love and grace as our foundation, let us press on with courage and determination, knowing that the steep climb of love's challenges will only strengthen our bond.

Chapter 3: Letter 10: The Steep Climb – Scaling Love's Challenges (cont.)

I love you deeply, and I am grateful for your forgiveness and understanding. Together, let us embrace the climb ahead, knowing that with God's guidance, we can overcome anything that stands in our way.

With a humble and contrite heart,
[Your Name]

Chapter 4:
Commitment - The Promise of Love

Introduction

Chapter 4 of our love story delves into the theme of commit-ment, exploring the profound promise that lies at the heart of a strong, and enduring relationship. In this chapter, we witness the power of unwavering love, the strength of shared vows, and the beauty of a steadfast bond.

Throughout the letters in this chapter, we explore the different facets of commitment in a marriage. From the binding thread that ties our love together, to the lighthouse that guides us on our journey, and the unbroken circle that symbolizes the continuity of our love, each letter showcases the depth, and significance of our commitment to one another.

We embrace the role of Christ as the cornerstone of our relationship, the anchor that provides stability in times of uncertainty, and the shining beacon that illuminates our path. With God as our foundation, we navigate the challenges of life, knowing that His love and guidance will lead us to a future filled with hope and purpose.

In this chapter, we express our gratitude for the unending melody that our love creates, the lasting impression we leave on each other's hearts, and the pledge of love that we make to each other. We recognize that our commitment is not simply a contract but a lifelong promise to stand by each other's side, through thick and thin.

As we journey through the pages of this chapter, we are reminded of the importance of having a strong spiritual partnership. We celebrate the joys of a love rooted in faith, and the blessings that come from seeking God's presence together. We understand that our commitment goes beyond the earthly realm, as we navigate our future hand in hand, guided by the love and grace of our Lord.

Chapter 4 is a testament to the power of commitment, the beauty of a love that endures, and the promise that we make to each other. It is a chapter filled with deep appreciation, heartfelt devotion, and a profound sense of gratitude for the love that we share. As we continue to explore the depths of commitment, we are reminded of the extraordinary journey we are on, and the incredible blessings that come from building a life together, rooted in love and faith.

May our commitment to one another continue to strengthen and deepen, as we embrace the promise of love that binds us together.

Chapter 4: Commitment - The Promise of Love

Letter 1: "The Binding Thread - Tying Our Love Together"
Letter 2: "The Lighthouse - Guiding Our Love's Journey" Letter 3: "The Unbroken Circle - The Continuity of Our Love"
Letter 4: "The Steadfast Stone - Our Unwavering Commitment"
Letter 5: "The Shining Beacon - Our Promise Illuminating the Path"

Letter 6: "The Anchor - Our Love's Stability"
Letter 7: "The Unending Melody - Our Love's Eternal Song"
Letter 8: "The Lasting Impression - The Mark of Our Love"
Letter 9: "The Oath - Our Pledge of Love"
Letter 10: "The Love's Compass - Navigating Our Future
Together"

Chapter 4: Letter 1: The Binding Thread – Tying Our Love Together

My Dearest [Husband's Name],

As I sit down to pen this letter, my heart is overfilled with love for you. In the depths of my soul, I am reminded of the beautiful thread that binds our hearts together, weaving a tapestry of love, commitment, and unwavering devotion. Today, I write to express my deep appreciation for the unbreakable bond we share, the binding thread that ties our love together.

When I reflect on the foundation of our love, I am reminded of the words from Ecclesiastes 4:12: "Though one may be overpowered, two can defend themselves. A cord of three strands is not quickly broken." It is through our commitment to each other and our faith in Jesus Christ that our love finds its strength and resilience. Like a thread that weaves through the fabric of our lives, our love is intertwined with the divine presence, and creating a bond that is unyielding and enduring.

In the journey of our love, I am continuously inspired by the words of 1 Corinthians 13:4-8, which beautifully describe the essence of love: "Love is patient, love is kind. It does not envy, it does not boast, it is not proud. It does not dishonor others, it is not self-seeking, it is not easily angered, it keeps no record of wrongs. Love does not delight in evil but rejoices with the truth. It always protects, always trusts, always hopes, always perseveres. Love never fails." These verses encapsulate the depth of my feelings for you and the commitment I hold in my heart.

My beloved, I want you to know that the thread that binds us is not simply a symbol but a testament to the promises we have made to each other. It is a reminder of the love that flows between us, the trust that grounds us, and the faith that sustains us. Through the highs and lows of life, we have remained steadfast, supporting and uplifting each other with unwavering devotion.

Today, I recommit myself to you, my beloved, with a renewed sense of love and affection. Let us continue to nurture our bond, sowing seeds of understanding, kindness, and forgiveness. Together, we will weather any storm that comes our way, for our love is fortified by the threads of commitment and the grace of God.

In your arms, I find solace, in your love, I find strength, and in your presence, I find home. As we continue this beautiful journey of love, may the binding thread that ties us together grow stronger with each passing day.

Forever yours,
[Your Name]

Chapter 4: Letter 2: The Lighthouse – Guiding Our Love's Journey

My Dearest [Husband's Name],

As I sit here to write this letter, my heart leaps with joy for the divine presence that illuminates our love's journey. Today, I want to express my deepest appreciation for the role that our Lord Jesus Christ plays as the guiding lighthouse in our lives, shining His light upon our path and leading us through the joys and challenges of marriage.

In the vast ocean of life, our love stands tall, and steadfast guided by the light of the lighthouse. It is through our shared faith and unwavering commitment to Christ that our love finds its true purpose and meaning. Just as a lighthouse guides ships safely to the shore, our Lord guides our hearts, and directs our steps ensuring that we navigate the waters of life with wisdom, love, and compassion.

The beauty of our relationship lies in our shared connection to the divine. It is the blessing of God's presence that empowers and sustains our marriage, filling it with light, love, hope, and all the wonderful attributes of our Lord Jesus Christ. In His presence, we find solace, strength, and the unwavering support to face any storm that may arise.

As I reflect on the words of Psalm 119:105: "Your word is a lamp for my feet, a light on my path," I am reminded of how God's Word serves as the eternal beacon that guides us in our journey together. It is through His teachings and commandments that we navigate the complexities of life, always seeking to honor, and love one another as He loves us.

My love, I am truly blessed to walk this journey hand in hand with you, knowing that our hearts are equally yoked and our spirits united in Christ. Together, we are anchored in His Love, guided by His Wisdom, and protected by His Grace. The lighthouse of our Lord's presence shines brightly upon us, casting away the darkness and illuminating our path with hope and purpose.

In this shared journey, let us continue to cultivate a deep sense of gratitude and reverence for the role that our Lord plays in our lives and in our marriage. May His light continue to guide us, reminding us of the depth of His love and the boundless possibilities that lie ahead.

I thank you for being my beloved partner, and I am filled with joy and hope as we continue to navigate this love's journey together, guided by the eternal light of our Lord Jesus Christ.

Yours in love and faith,
[Your Name]

Chapter 4: Letter 3: The Unbroken Circle – The Continuity of Our Love

My Dearest [Husband's Name],

As I compose this letter to you, I am filled with a sense of wonder and deep appreciation for the unbroken circle of love that binds us together. It symbolizes the enduring commitment that we have made to each other and the profound significance of our love story.

Just as a circle has no beginning or end, our love knows no bounds. It is a continuous journey, marked by relentless dedication, steadfast support, and an unbreakable bond. Our love has weathered storms and celebrated triumphs always remaining strong and resilient.

In the tapestry of our lives, every thread of commitment weaves together to form this unbroken circle. It signifies the promises we made to one another, the vows we exchanged on our wedding day, and the sacred commitment we hold in our hearts. It is a testament to the power of our love, rooted in trust, respect, and unwavering devotion.

Our love's continuity lies in our unwavering commitment to one another. We choose to show up for each other, and to be present in both the joys and the challenges of life. It is in our commitment that we find strength, stability, and a sense of purpose. Through the highs and lows, we remain steadfast knowing that our love is an anchor that keeps us grounded.

As we journey together, I am reminded of the words from Ecclesiastes 4:12: "Though one may be overpowered, two can defend themselves. A cord of three strands is not quickly broken." Our commitment to each other is fortified by our shared faith in God, and it is this divine partnership that gives our love an unshakeable foundation.

My love, I want you to know that how deeply grateful I am for the commitment we share. It is the fuel that keeps our love burning brightly, even in the face of challenges. I am thankful for your unwavering dedication, your willingness to weather storms by my side, and your relentless pursuit of our shared dreams.

Let us celebrate the unbroken circle of our love, cherishing each moment and embracing the future with hope and joy. Together, we will continue to strengthen this circle, knowing that our commitment is the cornerstone upon which our love thrives.

With a heart full of love and gratitude, I am honored to walk this journey with you, my beloved. May our love's continuity inspire others, and may it be a beacon of hope and joy in a world that often seeks to break the bonds of love.

Yours in love and commitment,
[Your Name]

Chapter 4: Letter 4: The Steadfast Stone – Our Unwavering Commitment

My Dearest [Wife's Name],

As I write these words, my heart overflows with warmth and affection for the depth and unwavering commitment that binds us together. It is a joy and a blessing to journey through life with you, my beloved wife, as we walk hand in hand, guided by the light of our Lord Jesus Christ.

In the depths of my soul, I am filled with awe and adoration for you, my beloved wife. Your beauty, both inward and outward, radiates the love and light of Christ. Your unwavering commitment to our marriage and your relentless pursuit of a relationship with our Savior blesses my life beyond measure.

Ephesians 2:20 reminds us that we are built on the foundation of the apostles and prophets, with Christ Jesus Himself as the chief cornerstone. Our love is rooted in this unshakable foundation, firmly established in the love and grace of our Lord. It is through His strength that our commitment remains unyielding.

In you, I see a reflection of God's love and grace. Your heart is steadfast, your faith unwavering. It is a joy to walk this journey of life with you, knowing that our commitment is not based on fleeting emotions but on the eternal promise we made before God.

Our commitment is more than a mere contract; it is a covenant of love, and a promise to honor and cherish one another as Christ loves the church. I am humbled and grateful that we are equally yoked, not only soulmates but spiritmates seeking the Lord's guidance and wisdom in every decision we make.

As we navigate the joys and challenges of life, we can take solace in the fact that our commitment is rooted in the unchanging love of Jesus Christ. His presence in our marriage is a guiding light, illuminating our path and infusing our relationship with hope, joy, and resilience.

I am honored to be your husband, to share in the joys and trials of life, and to witness your unwavering faith in our Savior. Your love for Jesus shines brightly, illuminating the path for the both of us. Together, we are on a journey of growth, deepening our commitment, and strengthening our bond in the love of Christ.

My beloved, I cherish you with all my heart. Our commitment to one another is a testament to the incredible gift we have been given. As we continue this journey, let us always hold fast to our faith in Christ, knowing that His love will guide us through every season of our lives.

With a heart full of love,
[Your Name]

Chapter 4: Letter 5: The Shining Beacon – Our Promise Illuminating the Path

My Dearest [Husband's Name],

My love, my heart brims with gladness for the incredible man you are and the immense love we share. You are not just my husband but my partner, soulmate, and spiritual companion. Your commitment to seeking God's wisdom and presence daily has illuminated our path, making you a shining beacon in our relationship.

In this chapter of our love story, titled "The Shining Beacon: Our Promise Illuminating the Path," I want to express my deepest gratitude for having such an amazing man by my side. Your unwavering faith and dedication to seeking God's wisdom and presence daily have been a guiding light in our relationship.

Proverbs 4:18: "But the path of the righteous is like the light of dawn, which shines brighter and brighter until full day." This verse reminds me of our promise to one another, rooted in the love of Christ, has become a shining beacon that guides us through the twists and turns of life. It is a constant reminder of the commitment we have made to each other, to God, and to the beautiful journey we are on together.

Your love encompasses every aspect of our lives, from the simple moments of laughter and joy to the challenges we face with strength and perseverance. I am grateful for the way you hold my hand through both the brightest and darkest of times, always reminding me of the light that shines within us.

In your arms, I find solace and comfort, knowing that we are united in our faith and our love for our Savior. The light of Christ radiates through you, casting out darkness and filling our lives with hope, compassion, and understanding. I am forever grateful to walk this path with you, hand in hand, as we navigate life's joys and trials.

My love for you deepens with each passing day, as we continue to grow together in the love of Christ. You are my anchor, my support, and my greatest blessing. I cherish the way you reflect Christ's love in our relationship and how you lead our family with humility and grace.

Thank you for being the shining beacon in my life, illuminating our path with your love, and devotion. As we continue this journey, I pledge to stand by your side, to support, and love you unconditionally, and to always seek God's wisdom as we navigate life together.

With all my heart,
[Your Name]

Chapter 4: Letter 6: The Anchor – Our Love's Stability

My Dearest [Husband's Name],

As I sit here reflecting on the journey of our love, I am reminded of the unwavering stability that you bring to our lives. You are the anchor that keeps us grounded, providing strength and security even in the midst of life's storms. This letter is a testament to the steadfastness and stability that our love brings, anchored in the foundation of Christ.

Just as an anchor holds a ship steady amidst the raging sea, you provide a sense of stability and assurance in our marriage. Your unwavering commitment and love act as a steadfast anchor, keeping us grounded and secure.

In the book of Hebrews, we are reminded of the hope we have in Christ as an anchor for our souls: "We have this hope as an anchor for the soul, firm, and secure" (Hebrews 6:19). Our love is anchored in the faith we share and the unbreakable bond we have in Christ. With Him as our foundation, our love is unshakable and enduring.

Your presence in my life is a constant source of strength and stability. Through the ups and downs, the uncertainties and challenges, you remain a steady force that I can always rely on. Your commitment to our marriage and your unwavering love for me provide a sense of security that I cherish deeply.

Just as an anchor provides stability and prevents a ship from drifting, our love keeps us centered, and aligned with God's purpose for our lives. It is through our love and partnership that we navigate the waters of life, knowing that we can weather any storm together.

As I think about our love story, I am filled with gratitude for the stability you bring to our relationship. Your love is not fleeting or temporary; it is solid and enduring. It is a love that weathers the trials and stands strong in the face of adversity. I am grateful for the comfort and security I find in your arms, knowing that our love is an anchor that holds us close.

Thank you for being the anchor in our lives, for providing stability, and for being my rock. I am honored and blessed to journey through life with you, knowing that our love is unbreakable and secure.

With all my heart,
[Your Name]

Chapter 4: Letter 7: The Unending Melody – Our Love's Eternal Song

My Dearest [Husband's Name],

As I sit here with pen in hand, my heart overflows with a melody that can only be described as the sweetest song of love. This letter is a testament to the unending melody that resonates in our hearts, the eternal song that weaves through the tapestry of our lives. You are my partner in this symphony, and together, we create a harmonious melody that echoes through eternity.

Our love is not confined by time or circumstance; it transcends the boundaries of this world and finds its home in the heavens above. It is an eternal song that grows more beautiful with each passing day.

In the book of Psalms, we find these words: "Sing to the Lord a new song; sing to the Lord, all the earth. Sing to the Lord, praise his name; proclaim his salvation day after day" (Psalm 96:1-2). Our love is a testament to God's faithfulness and the gift of His grace. It is a melody of praise, a song that proclaims His love and salvation in our lives.

Just as a beautiful melody can stir our hearts and bring tears to our eyes, our love resonates deeply within us. It is a song of joy, peace, and unfathomable beauty. It is a song that speaks of devotion, sacrifice, and unwavering commitment. It is a song that knows no end.

There is a Christian song that beautifully captures the essence of our love. It says, "In Christ alone, my hope is found; He is my light, my strength, my song." This song reminds us that our love is anchored in Christ, the source of all love and the author of our eternal song. With Him as our foundation, our melody will continue to play, and growing sweeter with each passing year.

As we walk hand in hand on this journey, my heart overflows with the melody that we create together. Your love brings harmony to my soul, and your presence is a soothing balm that brings peace and joy to my heart. I am grateful for every note we have shared, every verse we have written, and every chorus we have sung.

Together, let us continue to embrace the unending melody of our love, allowing it to guide us through the highs and lows of life. Let us sing our song with joy and gratitude, knowing that our love is a reflection of God's love for us.

With all my heart,
[Your Name]

Chapter 4: Letter 8: The Lasting Impression – The Mark of Our Love

My Dearest [Husband's Name],

As I reflect on our journey together, I am overwhelmed with deep appreciation and love for you. You are not just my husband but my soulmate and spiritual partner. Our connection goes beyond the surface, reaching the depths of our souls, and leaving a lasting impression that marks our love.

You have left an indelible mark on my heart, and our love has left an imprint that can never be erased. Your love has shaped me, molded me, and transformed me into the person I am today.

In the book of Song of Solomon, we read, "Set me as a seal upon your heart, as a seal upon your arm, for love is strong as death, jealousy is fierce as the grave. Its flashes are flashes of fire, the very flame of the Lord" (Song of Solomon 8:6). Our love is a seal upon our hearts, a bond that cannot be broken. It is a flame that burns with passion and devotion, leaving an everlasting mark on our souls.

You have touched my life in ways words cannot fully express. Your love has brought me comfort in times of sorrow, strength in moments of weakness, and joy in every season. The mark of your love is evident in the way you care for me, support me, and cherish our relationship.

I am grateful for the way you love me unconditionally, seeing the beauty within me even when I struggle to see it myself. Your love has taught me to love myself more deeply and to embrace the unique person God created me to be.

The mark of our love is not just seen in the big gestures or grand moments but also in the everyday acts of kindness and thoughtfulness. It is the way you hold my hand, listen to my heart, and make me feel cherished. It is the way you prioritize our relationship and continually strive to strengthen our bond.

You have shown me the depths of love and the true meaning of commitment. With you, I have experienced a love that surpasses all expectations and a bond that grows stronger with each passing day. Our love is a testimony to the faithfulness of God and the power of a covenant relationship.

As I look back on our journey together, I am in awe of the mark our love has left on my life. It is a mark of deep connection, unwavering support, and unending love. I am forever grateful for the lasting impression you have made on my heart.

With all my love,
[Your Name]

Chapter 4: Letter 9: The Oath – Our Pledge of Love

My Dearest [Wife's Name],

As I pen these words, I am filled with such a thankful heart for the incredible journey we have embarked upon together. Our path of love has led us through joys and challenges, triumphs and tribulations, and has shaped our commitment to one another.

Today, I want to assure you that I have spent time in prayer, speaking with God about your dreams and aspirations. I believe wholeheartedly that God has great plans for you and that He will help bring your dreams to fruition. I want to encourage you, my love, to keep dreaming big, for with God by our side, all things are possible.

As we continue on this path, we will encounter trials and challenges but our commitment binds us together. It is a pledge of love, an oath to support and uplift one another, to weather any storm that comes our way, and to continually strive for growth and unity in our marriage.

Together, let us walk this path with unwavering commitment, knowing that our love is anchored in God's unchanging love for us. As we face the unknown, may we hold onto the assurance that our love will guide us through every season of life.

I am forever grateful to have you as my beloved wife, my partner in life, and my soulmate. You are a source of inspiration and joy, and I am honored to walk alongside you on this beautiful path, bound by our sacred bond.

With all my love,
[Your Name]

Chapter 4: Letter 10: The Love's Compass – Navigating Our Future Together

My Dearest [Husband's Name],

As I sit down to write this letter to you, my heart is overflowing with love and appreciation for the incredible man that you are. You have been my rock, my partner, and my guiding light on this beautiful journey of life.

In this letter, I want to express my gratitude for the way you have navigated our future together. You have been a steady compass, always pointing us in the right direction, leading us towards a future filled with love, hope, and purpose.

It is such a blessing to have a husband who not only loves and supports me but also seeks the Lord in every aspect of our lives. We are able to approach God in prayer, not only individually but also together as a couple. Our shared faith strengthens our bond and fills our hearts with peace and joy.

I am grateful for the depth of our connection and the way we can relate to our Creator in various roles. He is our Elder, guiding us with His wisdom. He is our Brother, offering His love and support. He is our Spiritual Anchor, keeping us grounded. He is the Captain of our souls, leading us through the storms of life. And He is our Friend, always ready to listen and comfort us. Truly, He is the true lover of our souls.

The Bible serves as our blueprint for love in our relationship. It is a guide that illuminates the path we should walk, reminding us of the importance of love, forgiveness, and grace. It is a treasure that we can turn to for wisdom and guidance, as we seek to build a strong and lasting marriage.

As we navigate our future together, I want you to know how deeply I love and appreciate you. Your unwavering commitment, your strength, and your devotion inspire me every day. I am grateful for the love we share and the beautiful life we are building together.

May our love always be guided by the love of Christ, and may our future be filled with joy, adventures, and endless possibilities.

With all my love,
[Your Name]

Chapter 5: Resilience - The Strength of Love

Introduction

In Chapter 5, we delve into the theme of resilience within the realm of love. This section of the book explores the enduring power and strength of love in various contexts and circumstances. The letters within this chapter portray the unwavering commitment, adaptability, and tenacity that love brings forth.

As we journey through the letters in Chapter 5, we witness the remarkable ability of love to weather storms, overcome obstacles, and grow stronger through challenges. From heartfelt apologies to anniversary celebrations, these letters capture the essence of resilience in relationships.

The chapter reflects on the unyielding nature of love, its capacity to adapt and endure, and the bond that remains unbroken even in the face of adversity. It explores the deep connection between love and faith, highlighting the role of Christ as the source of strength and guidance in sustaining relationships.

Within these pages, readers will discover the beauty of love's persistence and its ability to bring healing, growth, and renewal. Each letter offers a unique perspective on the profound impact of resilience in nurturing and preserving love. The chapter serves as a testament to the power of love and its unwavering presence in the lives of those who embrace it.

As you immerse yourself in the letters of Chapter 5, prepare to be inspired by the resilience, strength, and enduring beauty of love. Allow these heartfelt expressions to resonate with your own experiences and kindle a deeper appreciation for the power of love to overcome, transform, and bring joy even in the most challenging times.

Chapter 5: Resilience - The Strength of Love

Letter 1: "The Bending Willow - Our Love's Flexibility"
Letter 2: "The Phoenix - Our Love Reborn From the Ashes"

Letter 3: "The Unbroken Chain - Our Love's Tenacity"
Letter 4: "The Evergreen - Our Love's Perpetual Vitality" Letter 5: "The Mighty Oak - Our Love's Strength"
Letter 6: "The Enduring Flame - Our Love's Persistent Glow"
Letter 7: "The Resilient Reed - Our Love's Capacity to Adapt"
Letter 8: "The Love's Armor - Protecting Our Sacred Bond"
Letter 9: "The Sturdy Shelter - Our Love's Refuge"
Letter 10: "The Unfading Bloom - Our Love's Timeless Beauty"

Chapter 5: Letter 1: The Bending Willow – Our Love's Flexibility

My Dearest [Husband's Name],

As we continue on this beautiful journey of love, I am filled with an overwhelming sense of admiration for the incredible man you are in my life. In this letter, I want to express my deep appreciation for your strength, intelligence, and the profound respect you have earned. However, what truly captivates my heart is your remarkable ability to be humble, loving, and flexible in our relationship.

The title of this letter, "The Bending Willow - Our Love's Flexibility," perfectly captures the essence of what I wish to convey. Like the graceful willow tree that sways with the wind, our love is rooted in the strength of our commitment, but it also possesses the remarkable quality of flexibility. It is this flexibility that allows us to navigate the challenges and changes that life presents us. We are not rigid, but rather, we bend and adapt with grace and understanding.

In the sacred bond of marriage, we are called to embody the spirit of humility and love. It is through our willingness to be flexible, to listen, and to understand each other's perspectives that our love flourishes. The Bible reminds us of the importance of flexibility in Proverbs 15:1, "A soft answer turns away wrath, but a harsh word stirs up anger." This verse reminds me of your gentle and patient nature, which has the power to

diffuse any tension and foster harmony in our relationship.
My love, I want you to know that I am blessed beyond measure to be your wife. You bring me a profound sense of peace and joy, and I am grateful that we walk this journey of life together. Your unwavering commitment to follow God's direction and your pursuit of His heart inspire me daily. I see His masterpiece in you, and I am in awe of the way you lead our family with wisdom and love.

In this letter, I want to affirm my love for you. I want to express my gratitude for your flexibility and the way you continuously strive to nurture our relationship. Your ability to humble yourself, to love deeply, and to be open to growth has created a bond that is unbreakable. I cherish the moments we share, the laughter we embrace, and the dreams we build together.

My love for you knows no bounds, and I am committed to walking hand in hand with you, embracing the challenges and joys that lie ahead. You are the anchor of my soul, and with you, I find the strength and courage to face any storm. Together, we bend and sway but we remain firmly rooted in our love.

Yours eternally,
[Your Name]

Chapter 5: Letter 2: The Phoenix – Our Love Reborn From the Ashes

My Dearest Wife,

Today, I want to express how blessed I feel to have you by my side, for you are like a phoenix, rising from the ashes, and bringing new life and hope into our relationship.

Throughout our journey together, we have faced challenges and obstacles that have tested our love and strength. But just like the phoenix, we have emerged stronger and more resilient. Your unwavering faith, your ability to rise above adversity, and your unwavering commitment to our love are truly inspiring.

I am humbled by the depth of your love and your ability to forgive and let go of the past. You have taught me the power of transformation and the beauty of second chances. In your presence, I feel reborn, ready to face each new day with hope and excitement.

Our love story is a testament to the incredible power of redemption and renewal. It is a reminder that even in the face of challenges and setbacks, we can find strength within ourselves and in our relationship. Together, we have the ability to overcome anything that comes our way and emerge stronger than ever.

I am grateful for every moment we have shared and for the love we continue to nurture and grow. You are the light that guides me, the fire that ignites my soul, and the love that brings me back to life. With you, I feel invincible, knowing that together, we can rise from any ashes and soar to new heights.

As we continue on this journey, I promise to always cherish and honor the love we share. Let us embrace the spirit of the phoenix, always willing to rise, renew, and rebuild. Our love story is a testament to the incredible power of transformation and the beauty that emerges from the ashes.

Forever and always, I am yours.

With all my love,
[Your Husband's Name]

Chapter 5: Letter 3: The Unbroken Chain – Our Love's Tenacity

My Dearest Husband,

As I reflect on our journey together, my heart overflows with appreciation for the unbreakable bond we share. Our love is like an unbroken chain, a testament to the tenacity that fuels our commitment to each other.

Through the twists and turns of life, we have remained steadfast, holding onto each other with resolute devotion. Our love has weathered storms, overcome challenges, and emerged even stronger. It is a chain that cannot be broken, binding us together in a bond that stands the test of time.

The tenacity of our love is a reflection of the deep connection we have nurtured over the years. We have chosen to love fiercely, to hold on tightly, and to never give up on each other. It is this enduring dedication that has carried us through the highs and lows, and it is what will continue to sustain us in the years to come.

In the face of adversity, we find solace in the knowledge that our love is unbreakable. Just as a chain is forged with unyielding strength, our commitment to each other is rooted in the foundation of trust, respect, and unwavering support. We have built something beautiful, something that endures.

Through this unbroken chain, we have learned the value of perseverance and the beauty of resilience. Our love's tenacity is a testament to the depth of our connection and the promise we made to one another.

Today, I want to express my deep appreciation for the love we share and the unbroken chain that binds us together. You are my partner, my confidant, and my rock. I am grateful for your constant presence in my life, for your love that knows no bounds.

In the years ahead, I know that we will face new challenges and embrace new adventures. But with the unbroken chain of our love, we can navigate any storm, overcome any obstacle, and emerge stronger than ever before. Our love's tenacity is our guiding light, reminding us of the unbreakable bond we have formed.

As we walk this path together, I am reminded of the words in Ephesians 4:2: "with all humility and gentleness, with patience, bearing with one another in love," These words teach us to hold each other up in love, with humility, patience, and gentleness.

Chapter 5: Letter 3: The Unbroken Chain – Our Love's Tenacity (cont.)

Furthermore, Galatians 6:9 reminds us to "not become weary in doing good, for at the proper time we will reap a harvest if we do not give up." This verse serves as a reminder to persevere in our love, even when faced with challenges, knowing that our dedication and efforts will bear fruit in due time.

Thank you, my love, for being the anchor in my life, for embracing the challenges with me, and for never letting go of our love. Together, we will continue to walk this path, hand in hand, knowing that the unbroken chain of our love will lead us to a future filled with joy, growth, and endless possibilities.

With all my heart,
[Your Wife's Name]

Chapter 5: Letter 4: The Evergreen – Our Love's Perpetual Vitality

My Dearest [Husband's Name],

As I sit here, reflecting on the beautiful journey of our love, I am reminded of the evergreen, a symbol of eternal life and perpetual vitality. Our love, like the resilient evergreen, possesses a strength that withstands the tests of time and the changing seasons of life. It is a testament to the boundless love and grace of our Lord Jesus Christ, who is the source of all life and vitality.

In His Word, we find comfort and guidance, and it is through His love that our love finds its eternal source. Just as the evergreen remains evergreen, our love is sustained by the everlasting presence of our Savior. His love permeates every aspect of our relationship, infusing it with beauty, resilience, and vitality.

In Colossians 3:14, we are reminded of the importance of love in our lives: "And over all these virtues put on love, which binds them all together in perfect unity." It is this binding love, grounded in Christ's example that fortifies our commitment to one another and brings perpetual vitality to our marriage.

Through His love, we find the strength to weather storms, to embrace growth, and to remain steadfast in our devotion. The love of Christ is the cornerstone of our union, providing a firm foundation upon which our relationship thrives.

As we journey through life together, I am grateful for the abiding presence of Jesus in our lives. He is the wellspring of joy, the source of grace, and the giver of eternal life. In Him, we find the everlasting love that breathes life into our love story, allowing it to flourish and endure.

I cherish every moment spent with you, my beloved. You are the embodiment of God's love in my life, and I am forever grateful for the vitality and beauty our love shares. May we continue to walk hand in hand, rooted in Christ's love, and may our love forever be an evergreen testimony of His faithfulness.

With all my love and devotion,
[Your Wife's Name]

Chapter 5: Letter 5: The Mighty Oak – Our Love's Strength

My Dearest [Wife's Name],

As we continue on this beautiful journey of love, I am in awe of the strength and vitality that our love embodies. Just like the Mighty Oak, our love stands tall and unwavering, rooted in the deep foundation of our faith in Christ.

In Psalm 18:2, it says, "The Lord is my rock, my fortress, and my deliverer; my God is my rock, in whom I take refuge, my shield and the horn of my salvation, my stronghold." This verse reminds me of the strength we find in God and how He is the solid foundation of our love. With Him as our rock, we can weather any storm that comes our way.

You, my beloved, are the epitome of strength and grace. Your unwavering faith in God and your steadfast commitment to our relationship inspire me every day. I am grateful for the love and support you bring into my life, and I cherish the unbreakable bond we share.

Our love is like the branches of the Mighty Oak, reaching out and growing stronger with each passing day. It is a testament to the faithfulness and love of our Savior, Jesus Christ. He is the source of our love's vitality, and through Him, our love remains evergreen and resilient.

In your presence, I find solace and peace. Your love breathes life into my soul, and I am grateful for the way you walk alongside me in this journey of life. Together, we are an unbroken chain, connected by love and committed to the well-being of each other.

My prayer for us is that we continue to draw strength from the Mighty Oak, who is Christ, and that our love remains steadfast and full of vitality. May our love be a beacon of hope and inspiration to others, as we navigate the joys, and challenges of life together.

I am honored to be your husband and to share this incredible love with you. You are my rock, my partner, and my best friend. With you by my side, I know that our love will endure and thrive, like the Mighty Oak, for all eternity.

Forever and always,
[Your Husband's Name]

Chapter 5: Letter 6: The Enduring Flame – Our Love's Persistent Glow

My Dearest [Husband's Name],

As we journey through the pages of our love story, I am filled with genuine thankfulness for the enduring flame that burns within our hearts. Today, I write to you, my beloved, to celebrate the persistent glow of our love that is fueled by the power of Christ in us.

In this chapter of our lives, I am amazed by the personal and intimate relationship you have with the Lord. Your dedicated devotion and steadfast faith have become a source of inspiration for me. I cherish the moments we spend together, abiding in Christ and soaking in His presence. It is in those moments that our love is refined and strengthened, radiating a glow that shines brightly even in the darkest of times.

Delighting ourselves in the Lord has truly granted us the desires of our hearts, for our hearts are rejoicing in our salvation. No matter the circumstances we face, we find solace in the knowledge that Jesus is the source of our joy. We sing praises to His name, lifting our voices in unison as a testament to the love and grace that flows through our lives.

My love, you are the enduring flame that warms my soul and ignites my spirit. The glow of our love is not merely a flickering flame, but a persistent and steadfast light that illuminates our journey together. It is a love that reflects the love of Christ, a love that endures and stands firm in the face of trials.

With each passing day, I am reminded of the depth of our bond and the blessings we share as husband and wife. The flame of our love continues to burn brightly, drawing others to the warmth and beauty of our relationship. I am grateful beyond words for the love we share and the profound impact it has on our lives.

May our love always be a reflection of Christ's love for us, a love that knows no bounds and perseveres through all circumstances. Together, let us continue to nurture the enduring flame, basking in its radiant glow and spreading its warmth to those around us.

Yours forever and always,
[Your Name]

Chapter 5: Letter 7: The Resilient Reed – Our Love's Capacity to Adapt

My Dearest [Husband's Name],

As I sit here reflecting on the journey of our love, I am amazed by the capacity we have to adapt and grow, much like the resilient reed that sways with the winds of change. Today, I pen this letter to you, pouring out my heart in a way I have never expressed before.

From the moment our paths intertwined, I knew that our love was destined to be a beautiful testament to the grace and mercy of our Lord. Through the seasons of life, we have faced challenges, storms, and uncertainties, but our love has remained steadfast and unwavering.

Like the reed that bends without breaking, we have learned to adapt and embrace the changes that come our way. Our love has the remarkable ability to withstand the trials and tribulations, growing stronger with each experience. It is a testament to the power of faith and the love that binds us together.

In your arms, I find solace and strength. Your reliable support and unwavering faith in God have carried us through the darkest of times. Your love has been the constant that grounds me, providing the stability and reassurance I need.

As I reflect on the beauty of our relationship, I am reminded of the verse from Isaiah 43:2: "When you pass through the waters, I will be with you; and when you pass through the rivers, they will not sweep over you. When you walk through the fire, you will not be burned; the flames will not set you ablaze." Our love has endured the waters and the fires, emerging stronger, and more resilient each time.

I am grateful for the ways in which our love has adapted and grown. It is a reflection of our commitment to one another and our shared faith in God. Together, we have weathered storms, celebrated victories, and supported one another through it all.

My love for you knows no bounds. You are the rock upon which our love is built, and I am blessed beyond measure to have you by my side. As we continue this journey, I promise to adapt and grow alongside you, always seeking God's guidance and grace.

You are my partner, my confidant, and my best friend. With you, I feel safe to embrace change and step into the unknown, for I know that our love will remain constant. I am forever grateful for the capacity our love has to adapt and thrive.

Yours eternally,
[Your Name]

Chapter 5: Letter 8: The Love's Armor – Protecting Our Sacred Bond

My Dearest [Husband's Name],

As I sit here, penning these words with a heart heavy with remorse, I kneel before the Lord, seeking His forgiveness and guidance. There are no words to adequately express the depth of my regret for the things I have said and done, for the pain I have caused you.

In moments of anger and frustration, my words were sharp and thoughtless. I lashed out without considering the impact on your gentle being and the tenderness of your heart. I am deeply sorry for the hurt I have caused, and I humbly ask for your forgiveness.

The love we share is a sacred bond, a treasure that must be protected at all costs. It is in this realization that I turn to the Lord and put on the armor of His protection. As I reflect on Ephesians 6:11-13, I am reminded of the importance of standing firm in the face of spiritual battles: "Put on the full armor of God, so that you can take your stand against the devil's schemes. For our struggle is not against flesh and blood, but against the rulers, against the authorities, against the powers of this dark world and against the spiritual forces of evil in the heavenly realms. Therefore, I put on the full armor of God, so that when the day of evil comes, you may be able to stand your ground."

With the strength and guidance of the Holy Spirit, I recognize the areas in which I need to grow. I am committed to making changes, to being more mindful of my words and actions, and to prioritizing our love above all else. I believe that the Lord can work miracles within us, healing our wounds and strengthening our bond.

In this journey of forgiveness and growth, I ask for your patience and understanding. I know that rebuilding trust takes time, but I am willing to fight for our marriage. I promise to seek the Lord's wisdom and guidance each day, relying on His grace to transform me into the woman you deserve.

Please know that my love for you is unconditional. You are the compass that directs my path, and I am eternally grateful for your presence in my life. Together, with the Lord as our guide and protector, we can overcome any obstacle that comes our way.

As I lay my heart bare before you, I pray that you find it in your heart to forgive me. Let us move forward hand in hand, protecting our sacred bond and allowing the love's armor to shield us from the storms that may come.

With all the love in my heart,
[Your Name]

Chapter 5: Letter 9: The Sturdy Shelter – Our Love's Refuge

My Dearest [Wife's Name],

As I pour out my heart onto this paper, I am filled with a deep sense of remorse and sorrow for the distance that has grown between us. I have allowed myself to become lost in the world, distracted by the schemes of the enemy, and I have strayed from the path of honesty and love that we once shared.

In moments of weakness, I allowed the fiery darts of the enemy to penetrate my heart and cloud my judgment. I became absent and disconnected, failing to show you the love and attention that you deserve. For this, I am truly sorry, and I ask for your forgiveness.

As I reflect on our early days together, I am reminded of the joy we found in the Lord, seeking His presence every day and night. It was in those moments that we felt the safety of His refuge and experienced the fullness of His love. However, I allowed the cares of the world to blind me, and causing me to neglect the precious bond we share.

I am broken, my love, and I cry out to you, pleading for your forgiveness. I am ready to change, to realign my priorities, and to surrender to God's will. Through personal and intimate moments with the Lord, He has opened my heart and eyes to the depth of my mistakes. I am willing to cooperate with His transformative work within me, and I am committed to fighting for our marriage.

You are my sturdy shelter, my refuge in the storm. Your love has always been a source of strength and solace for me, and I long to return to the place of intimacy and trust that we once shared. I ask for your patience and under-standing as we navigate this season of restoration, for I believe that with the Lord as our guide, we can rebuild what has been broken.

Let us seek His presence together, drawing near to Him and to one another. May His love envelop us, restoring our hearts and renewing our commitment to each other. In His refuge, we will find the strength to overcome the challenges that lie ahead.

I am grateful for your love, forgiveness, and steadfast support. You are a precious gift in my life, and I cherish the love we have built together. Please know that I am fully committed to honoring our marriage and protecting the sacred bond we share.

With a repentant and hopeful heart,
[Your Name]

Chapter 5: Letter 10: The Unfading Bloom – Our Love's Timeless Beauty

My Dearest [Wife's Name],

As I write this letter, my heart is filled with both joy and longing. Today, on this special milestone, our 20th wedding anniversary, I find myself away on a business trip, unable to be by your side. But even in my physical absence, my heart overflows with genuine thankfulness for the remarkable journey we have embarked upon together.

In these 20 years, our love has blossomed into an unfading bloom, radiating a timeless beauty that transcends all challenges and trials. Life has never been easy for us but through it all, our love for each other and our unwavering devotion to the Lord Jesus Christ have been the anchors that have sustained us.

Today, as I reflect on the day we exchanged our vows, my heart is moved with tears. I am transported back to the beach, where the sunset painted the sky with vibrant hues and the ocean whispered its melodies of peace. Even strangers paused their activities to witness the profound love that filled the air. It was a moment where heaven and earth converged, and the presence of the Lord was palpable.

Twenty years have passed since that glorious day, and our love has grown deeper and stronger with each passing year. The challenges we have faced have only served to strengthen our bond and ignite a fire within us that cannot be extinguished. Together, we have weathered storms and celebrated triumphs, always standing united in our faith and love.

Today, my heart yearns to be with you, to hold you close, and to shower you with the love and affection that fills every fiber of my being. I cannot wait to return to your side, to embrace you with a passion that transcends words, and to share with you the surprise I have planned to celebrate this momentous occasion.

Understand that my love for you transcends all limits. You are the embodiment of beauty, grace, and strength. The laughter we have shared, the tears we have shed, and the memories we have created together are treasures that I will forever cherish.

As we enter this new chapter of our lives, I am filled with anticipation and excitement for what the Lord has in store for us. Our love story is far from over, and I am committed to making every moment count, cherishing, and nurturing the love that we have cultivated over the years.

On this anniversary, and every day that follows, let us celebrate the love that has stood the test of time, the love that is a reflection of the eternal love our Savior has for us. You are my forever, and I am grateful beyond words for the privilege of sharing this remarkable journey with you.

With all my love,
[Your Name]

Chapter 6:
Devotion - The Depth of Love

Introduction

In Chapter 6, we delve into the theme of devotion and explore the profound depth of love shared between the couple. This chapter showcases ten heartfelt letters that illustrate the power of unwavering commitment, spiritual connection, and the journey of love.

Within this section of the book, readers can expect to embark on an emotional journey, experiencing the various facets of devotion within a loving relationship. The letters capture the essence of a deep and abiding love, rooted in faith and guided by the principles of Christianity.

Each letter tells a unique story, unveiling the heartfelt emotions and expressions of love between the couple. From the constancy of love in "The Guiding North Star" to the depths of love in "The Deep Well," readers will witness the growth, challenges, and triumphs of a love that stands the test of time.

As readers progress through the letters, they will encounter themes such as the weaving of lives, the sanctity of devotion, the profound depths of love, and the endless journey of love. The letters offer glimpses into the couple's shared experiences, spiritual connection, and the ways in which they navigate the complexities of life hand in hand.

Through the exploration of devotion, readers will witness the power of love to transcend boundaries, endure trials, and inspire personal growth. The letters serve as a testament to the couple's unwavering commitment, their shared faith, and the transformative power of love in their lives.

In reading this chapter, readers are invited to reflect on their own relationships and discover the beauty and depth that can be found through devotion. Whether in the joyful moments or the challenges faced; these letters provide a glimpse into the power of love and the ways in which it can shape and enrich our lives.

Join us on this journey of devotion, as we dive into the depth of love and discover the transformative power that lies within.

Chapter 6: Devotion - The Depth of Love

Letter 1: "The Guiding North Star - Our Love's Constancy"
Letter 2: "The Love's Tapestry - Weaving Our Lives Together"
Letter 3: "The Deep Well - Our Love's Profound Depths" Letter 4: "The Sacred Altar - Our Love's Sacred Devotion"
Letter 5: "The Ocean's Mariana - The Deepest Point of Our Love"
Letter 6: "The Love's Symphony - Harmonious Connection"

Letter 7: "The Unending Voyage - Our Love's Endless Journey"
Letter 8: "The Eternal Flame - Our Love's Unfaltering Glow"
Letter 9: "The Deepest Dive - Submerging into Our Love"
Letter 10: "The Love's Echo - Resounding in Our Hearts"

Chapter 6: Letter 1: The Guiding North Star – Our Love's Constancy

My Dearest [Husband's Name],

As I sit down to write this letter, my heart overflows with love and gratitude for the guiding North Star that is our love's constancy. It is in the unyielding love of our Lord Jesus Christ that we find the foundation of our relationship, the source of our strength, and the guiding light that leads us through the highs and lows of life.

In a world where human love can be fickle, influenced by ever-changing emotions, we are blessed to have the constant love of our Savior to anchor our hearts. His love is not swayed by circumstances or fleeting feelings; it is steadfast, unchanging, and unconditional. It is this divine love that we look to as our North Star, guiding us in our journey together.

When we fix our gaze upon Jesus, when we abide in His peace and immerse ourselves in His presence, our love blossoms and flourishes. It is in those moments that we experience the power of the Holy Spirit working within us, filling our hearts with His love, and enabling us to love one another and others with an unbreakable, unshakable love.

My beloved, let us be a testament to the love that people have not seen before. Let us demonstrate through our actions, our words, and our commitment what it means to be guided by the North Star of Christ's love. May our love be a beacon of hope and inspiration to those around us, igniting a hunger in their hearts for the kind of love that God intended for marriages. The kind of love that is rooted in a shared faith, a commitment to following Him, and a dedication to living out His commandments.

I am grateful beyond words to have you as my partner on this journey. Together, let us continue to seek the guiding North Star, drawing closer to Him and to one another with each passing day. May our love shine brightly, guiding others to experience the depth and constancy of God's love.

With all my love,
[Your Name]

Chapter 6: Letter 2: The Love's Tapestry – Weaving Our Lives Together

My Dearest Love,

As I sit here and watch you enjoy the meal I have lovingly prepared for you, I am reminded of how our lives are intricately woven together, much like a beautiful tapestry. It is not just the food on your plate but a reflection of the depth of our love and the joy we find in serving one another.

With each slice of the knife, every stir of the spoon, and the careful seasoning, I have poured my heart into creating this meal for you. I want you to taste not just the flavors but also the love and devotion that went into every bite.

In the tapestry of our lives, you are the thread that weaves everything together. Our journey is a testament to the love and commitment we have for one another, and the way we navigate life hand in hand. We are not just two individuals but partners bound by a deep connection that surpasses words.

I am grateful for the way you lead our family with love and wisdom, always seeking to follow the guidance of our Lord. Your presence in my life brings me comfort, strength, and a sense of belonging. Together, we are creating a tapestry of love, faith, and shared experiences.

As we continue to weave our lives together, I am excited for the future that lies ahead. The tapestry we are creating is a reflection of God's grace and the beauty of our love.
With each passing day, I am reminded of how blessed I am to have you by my side.

Thank you, my love, for being the thread that holds our tapestry together. You are my anchor, my confidant, and my greatest source of joy. You are simply amazing. Let us continue to embrace the journey and cherish the moments that make our love story truly unique.

With all my love,
[Your Name]

Chapter 6: Letter 3: The Deep Well – Our Love's Profound Depths

My Sweetheart, My Love,

As I take this moment to reflect on our journey together, I am immensely thankful for the depth of love we share. Today, as we celebrate another year of marriage, the quiet dawn fills our home, creating a serene atmosphere that stirs my heart.

In this stillness, I am reminded of the profound depths of our love, and the love we have with our Lord Jesus Christ. I am thankful beyond words for the incredible person that you are, and for your unwavering understanding and acceptance of me, even in my less-than-pleasant moments. Your ability to see beyond my faults and love me unconditionally is a testament to the spiritual connection you have with the Holy Spirit.

Your relationship with God serves as a guiding light in your life, and it inspires me to seek a deeper connection with Him as well. I am in awe of the wisdom and understanding you possess, which can only be derived from spending intimate time with our Savior. Your encouragement, support, and laughter have become my refuge, and I am amazed by the strength of your faith.

As we continue on this journey together, I desire to grow even deeper in our love and in our love for Him. I long for more intimate moments of prayer, worship, and study where we can discover new depths of love and experience the fullness of His presence. I want to prioritize the eternal over the temporary, and to focus on the things that truly matter in our lives.

The Bible reminds us in 1 Corinthians 13:4-7, "Love is patient, love is kind. It does not envy, it does not boast, it is not proud. It does not dishonor others, it is not self-seeking, it is not easily angered, it keeps no record of wrongs. Love does not delight in evil but rejoices with the truth. It always protects, always trusts, always hopes, always perseveres."

In this journey of deepening love, I am grateful to have you by my side. Your unshakeable faith, your consistent support, and your unconditional love have shaped our relationship into something beautiful and profound. Let us continue to seek the depths of love together, as we grow in our love for one another and in our love for our Savior.

With all my heart and soul,
[Your Name]

Chapter 6: Letter 4: The Sacred Altar – Our Love's Sacred Devotion

My Dearest Pumpkin, My Love, and My Everything,

As I sit here in the quietness of our home, I'm reflecting on the sacred devotion we share. Our love is like a sacred altar, a place where we come together to offer our hearts, our lives, and our love to our Lord Jesus Christ.

In the midst of life's busyness and distractions, it is in this sacred space that we find solace and strength. We have built a foundation of love, trust, and faith, and we continually strive to honor and nurture it. Our commitment to each other and our commitment to our Savior have intertwined in creating a bond that is unbreakable.

Through the highs and lows, we have stood side by side, seeking His guidance, and leaning on His promises. Our love is not just a feeling or a fleeting emotion; it is a reflection of the sacred devotion we have for each other and for our Lord.

As we gather at the sacred altar of our love, we bring our joys, our fears, our dreams, and our prayers. We surrender ourselves to His will, knowing that His plans for us are far greater than anything we could ever imagine. Together, we offer our hearts and our lives as a testimony of His love and grace.

In Ephesians 5:25, it says, "Husbands, love your wives, just as Christ loved the church and gave himself up for her." These words remind me of the sacrificial love that Christ demonstrated for His bride, the church. It is through His example that we learn how to love selflessly, to lay down our lives for one another.

My beloved, I want you to know that I am committed to walking this sacred journey of love with you. I promise to honor, cherish, and uplift you as we navigate life together. Our love is a testament to the power of devotion and the beauty of a marriage centered on Christ.

Thank you for being my partner, my confidant, and my best friend. I am forever grateful for the sacred devotion we share, and I am filled with joy and anticipation for the journey that lies ahead.

Yours forever and always, loving you,
[Your Husband's Name]

Chapter 6: Letter 5: The Oceans Marina – The Deepest Point of Our Love

My Love, My Baby, My Blessing,

Today, as I reflect on the depths of our love, my heart is filled with a sense of awe and wonder. Our love is like the vastness of the ocean, with its hidden treasures and unexplored depths. It is in the Mariana Trench, the deepest point of the ocean, where our love reaches its greatest depth.

Just like the ocean, our love is filled with mystery, beauty, and endless possibilities. It is a love that surpasses human understanding and transcends the boundaries of time and space. Our love is a gift from above, a reflection of the love our Lord Jesus Christ has for us.

In the depths of the Mariana Trench, the pressure is immense, yet life thrives and remarkable creatures abound. Similarly, in the deepest parts of our love, we find resilience, strength, and a profound connection that withstands the trials of life. Our love is not defined by the shallow waters, but by the depths we are willing to explore together.

My darling, you are the anchor that keeps me grounded in the stormy seas of life. Your love is a beacon that guides me through the darkest nights. When I am lost in the depths of my own emotions, you are there to lift me up and remind me of the vastness of our love.

Just as the ocean waves crash against the shore, our love has weathered storms and challenges, but it has never wavered. It is in the Mariana Trench of our love that I find solace and peace, knowing that we are bound together by a love that is eternal and unbreakable.

I am grateful for the depths of our love, for the moments of vulnerability and intimacy we share. In your embrace, I find comfort and security, knowing that we are united not only in our love for each other but also in our love for our Savior.

As I look into your eyes, I see the reflection of a love that goes beyond the surface. It is a love that is built on a foundation of faith, trust, and commitment. Our love is an ocean, vast and ever-changing, yet constant in its power and beauty.

My love, I want you to know that I am here, ready to dive deeper into the ocean of our love. Together, let us explore the uncharted territories, discovering new depths, and experiencing the wonders of love. I cherish every moment we share, and I am grateful for the privilege of being your wife.

I love you always and forever,
Your Wife

Chapter 6: Letter 6: The Love's Symphony – Our Harmonious Connection

My dearest love,

As the moonlight softly illuminates our room, I find myself unable to contain the overwhelming love that fills my heart in this moment. It is in the stillness of the night that I am reminded of the incredible blessing it is to be married to you, my beloved wife. The depth of my emotions for you is immeasurable, and I am compelled to pour out my heart to you in this letter.

The love we share, my sweet, is like a symphony, each note perfectly harmonizing with the next. Our connection goes beyond mere words or gestures; it is a melody that resonates within our souls. In the quiet moments, I am reminded of the way our lives have intertwined, creating a beautiful composition that only God could have orchestrated.

With every sweet kiss, every tender touch against your soft skin, I am reminded of the depth of our love. Our love is not just a fleeting emotion; it is rooted in a foundation of trust, honesty, and vulnerability. The beauty of our relationship lies in our unwavering commitment to be open and transparent with each other, even in moments of vulnerability. It is in these moments that our love truly shines, strengthening the bond we share.

But my love, it is not only our love for each other that fills my heart with joy. It is also the love we both have for our Savior, Jesus Christ. Our shared devotion to Him has been the guiding force in our relationship, shaping our values, and deepening our love for one another. It is through His grace and love that we have found such an incredible connection, and for that, I am eternally grateful.

As I look around and take in the beauty of our harmonious connection, I am overwhelmed with a sense of profound gratitude. I know, without a doubt, that I am the most blessed person in the world to have you by my side. Our love is a gift, a treasure that we cherish with every beat of our hearts.

My love, thank you for being the melody that completes my life. I am forever grateful for the symphony of love that we share, and I am excited for the chapters yet to come in our love story.

With all my heart,
Your adoring husband

Chapter 6: Letter 7: The Unending Voyage – Our Love's Endless Journey

My dearest husband,

As we embark on yet another year of our unending voyage together, my heart is filled with overwhelming appreciation and love for the incredible man that you are. From the moment we set sail on this journey called marriage, you have been my constant companion, guiding me with your amazing love and support.

I want you to know, my love, how much I appreciate you for the person you are. You have a remarkable ability to navigate through life without getting caught up in worries over things that may never happen. You remind me time and time again that worrying will not change the outcome, and instead, you teach me to trust in God's providence. Your wisdom and perspective are invaluable, and I am grateful to have you by my side.

One of the things that I admire the most about you is how you sow seeds of love, friendship, and empathy wherever you go. Your kindness and genuine care for others make a lasting impact on those around you. You have a unique ability to make people laugh, to bring joy into their lives, and I am blessed to be the recipient of your infectious laughter and warm spirit.

I am in awe of your steadfast belief in me and your constant encouragement. You never fail to remind me of my strengths and capabilities, pushing me to reach new heights. Your belief in me gives me the strength and confidence to pursue my dreams and face challenges head-on. I am grateful beyond words for your dedicated and simply amazing support.

My love, you always ensure that I am aware of your appreciation for me, for the little things I do and the love I pour into our relationship. Your gratitude fills my heart and reminds me of the importance of expressing love and appreciation daily. I am reminded of how blessed I am to have you as my husband, and I thank God every day for the precious gift that you are.

I adore the way you open the door for me, a true gentleman in every sense. Your respect and value for me as your wife mean the world to me. Your role as a strong spiritual leader, always putting the Lord Jesus first in our lives, sets the foundation for our journey. It is through your example that I am inspired to seek God's guidance and make Him preeminent in every detail of our lives.

As we celebrate this special day of our anniversary, my heart spills over with tremendous love for you. Tears well up in my eyes as I reflect on the beautiful moments we have shared and the countless memories we have yet to create. This unending voyage we are on is filled with endless possibilities, and I am excited to navigate the waters of life together, hand in hand.

Forever grateful and deeply in love,
Your adoring wife

Chapter 6: Letter 8: The Eternal Flame – Our Love's Unfaltering Glow

My Dearest Love,

As we step into another phase of our shared journey, my heart is brimming with overwhelming appreciation for the love that exists between us - a love that flickers with an eternal glow, warming every crevice of my soul. The title I have chosen for this letter, "The Eternal Flame - Our Love's Unfaltering Glow," seeks to capture the essence of our enduring love, a love that has illuminated the darkest corners of our lives and continues to shine brighter with each passing moment.

Your unwavering optimism and resilience in the face of life's trials are nothing short of inspiring. You have shown me how to let go of unfounded fears, focusing instead on the blessings we have been bestowed. Your wisdom and inner strength have guided me towards a path of hope, encouraging me to trust in the Lord's divine plan.

Each day, I find myself becoming more grateful for the seeds of love, friendship, and understanding that you tirelessly sow into our relationship. Your readiness to lend a helping hand, your ability to bring laughter into my life when I need it most, and your unfaltering belief in me, even in moments of self-doubt, are gifts that I cherish deeply.

As we celebrate another year of our togetherness, my heart is flooded with a profound sense of gratitude for the incredible gift that you are in my life. I thank God each day for blessing me with a partner as genuine, loving, and faithful as you are. Your presence serves as a constant reminder of God's infinite grace and benevolence.

Your small gestures, like buying me flowers just because or your foot rubs when I am exhausted, are a testament to the deep respect and adoration you have for me. Your leadership, both in our spiritual journey and in our day-today life, is a shining example of your commitment to putting the Lord Jesus first in all things.

Reflecting on our shared journey, I find myself moved with tears by the depth of my love for you. Our love has only grown stronger with each passing day, filling me with anticipation for the future we are building together. I consider myself blessed beyond measure to have you by my side as my partner, my confidant, and my best friend.

Thank you for choosing me, for being my anchor in the tempestuous seas of life. Your love brings a sense of tranquility and joy to my soul, a feeling that words can hardly express. I eagerly await the countless adventures that lie ahead of us in this eternal journey of love.

With all my love,
Your Devoted Wife

Chapter 6: Letter 9: The Deepest Dive Submerging into Our Love

My Beloved,

Our journey together has been like a deep dive into an ocean of love, an ocean where each new depth reveals layers of compassion, understanding, and mutual respect that strengthen our bond. This is the "Deepest Dive - Submerging Into Our Love," a journey that we undertake every day, growing deeper and more profound with each passing moment.

My love, your unwavering devotion to the Lord and your relentless pursuit of His wisdom are traits that I not only admire but also strive to emulate. Your commitment to seeking the Lord first in everything you do is a testament to your faith and serves as a guiding beacon for our family. As Ecclesiastes 4:9-12 states, "Two are better than one… For if they fall, one will lift up his fellow. But woe to him who is alone when he falls and has not another to lift him up!" Your companionship, my love, has indeed made me stronger and more resilient.

One of the many gifts that our shared love has given me is the assurance of honesty and trust. Knowing that you are guided by the Lord's wisdom and are led along straight paths gives me an indescribable peace. I am continuously praying for your direction, not just in our relationship, but also in your walk with Christ Jesus.

Even when we walk through the valley of the shadow of death, as Psalm 23:4 states, I am confident that we will fear no evil, for the Lord is with us, and your rod and your staff, they comfort me. This faith we share, this common belief, only deepens my love for you and strengthens our bond.

Your heart, my love, is a treasure. It overflows with kindness towards me and devotion to the Lord. I cherish your gentleness, your patience, and your unwavering commitment to providing for our family. These are qualities that are rare to find, and I never take them for granted.

Each day, as I witness your love for me and for the Lord,
I am filled with a profound sense of awe and gratitude. This love, this divine gift we have been blessed with, is something I cherish deeply. Our journey, our deep dive into the ocean of love, has been the greatest adventure of my life, and I look forward to the depths we are yet to explore.

In this letter, and in every silent prayer, I thank God for the gift of you. You are my partner, my confidant, and my greatest blessing. As we continue our journey, our dive into the depths of our love, I am excited to see the treasures we will discover together.

With all my love,
Your Devoted Wife

Chapter 6: Letter 10: The Love's Echo Resounding in Our Hearts

My Dearest,

The quiet of the house is tangible as I pen these words, an echo of the absence your calling necessitates. The hush is not a void, but a reminder of the profound echo of your love that resides within these walls, within my heart. It is the quiet that you leave in your wake, not of emptiness but of anticipation, a love song waiting to be sung.

Today was one of those days, my love, where the sun rose and set without our paths crossing. The world needed you, as it often does, and as you always do, you responded with grace and dedication. Yet, as I sit here in our home, the aroma of the dinner I've prepared wafting through the air, I am not disheartened. I am instead filled with a profound sense of gratitude and admiration for you.

In the midst of our schedules and responsibilities, I see us not as two individuals pulled apart but as a testament of resilience, the embodiment of the commitment we made when we said 'I do.' In the face of our trials, we have become more than just a couple; we have become an emblem of enduring love and steadfast partnership.

Your selflessness, your dedication, and the sheer force of your love – it does not go unnoticed. Each patient you heal, each life you touch, it reflects back on us, on our love. It is an echo resounding in my heart, a testament to your unwavering strength and kindness. You are a beacon, my love, not only for me but for every life you touch. You are not just my wife, my partner, but a blessing that enriches all around you.

With each passing day, I find myself falling deeper in love with you, appreciating you more for not just who you are to me, but who you are to the world. The moments we share, the conversations we have, each one is a gem, a precious memory that strengthens and deepens our bond. Our time together may be limited, but it is profound, filled with a depth of love and understanding that transcends the ordinary.

Yes, the space between us is filled with challenges, the trials of time and distance. But I've come to see this not as a hurdle, but as a testament to our love. The pain of separation is but a shadow compared to the joy of our union. And so, every moment apart becomes a sweet anticipation of our reunion, a reminder of the depth of our love.

In writing this letter to you, my love, I hope you understand the depth of my affection, my admiration, my love for you. I want you to know that even in your absence, you are with me, always. Your love is my strength, your spirit my guiding star. And in your love, I find a joy and peace that surpasses the pain of our temporary separation.

Chapter 6: Letter 10: The Love's Echo Resounding in Our Hearts (cont.)

In the end, it is you and I, forever entwined, our love echoing across the distances, through the challenges, resounding in our hearts. Your love is my sanctuary, my refuge, my home.
And for that, I am eternally grateful.

With all my love,
[Your Name]

Chapter 7: Faith - The Divine Dimension of Love

Introduction

Welcome to Chapter 7 of "Letters of Love," where we embark on a journey into the depths of faith and the divine dimension of love. In this chapter, we delve into the sacred connection between love and belief, exploring the transformative power that faith brings to our relationships.

Within these pages, you will find ten beautifully crafted letters that capture the essence of a love deeply rooted in spiritual connection. Each letter serves as a testament to the profound impact that faith has on the love shared between two souls.

In this section of the book, we invite you to explore the intricacies of love intertwined with belief, as husband and wife express their devotion, reflect on the sanctity of their union, and seek solace in the arms of their Savior.

Through these letters, you will witness the beauty of love that transcends earthly boundaries, as the couples draw inspiration from sacred scriptures, rely on prayer as a guiding force, and find strength in the presence of the Lord.

The letters in this chapter will touch your heart, ignite your own faith, and inspire you to nurture a deeper spiritual connection in your own relationships. They speak of the unbreakable bond forged when two hearts unite in the shared belief and trust in a higher power.

As you journey through these pages, you will be reminded of the beauty of a love that is grounded in faith, and the transformative power it holds. You will witness how the love between two individuals can be strengthened, enriched, and made holy through their unwavering commitment to God.

May these letters serve as a guiding light, illuminating the path towards a love that is rooted in the divine. May they inspire you to seek a deeper spiritual connection in your own relationships, allowing your love to flourish and radiate the light of faith.

Open your heart and let the words within these letters resonate within you. May they remind you of the infinite possibilities that unfold when love and faith intertwine, creating a bond that is truly sacred, and enduring.

Enjoy this remarkable journey through the realm of faith, as love finds its ultimate purpose and meaning in the divine dimension. May you be inspired, encouraged, and forever changed by the profound depth of love rooted in faith.

With love and blessings,
Sylwia Mills

Chapter 7: Faith - The Divine Dimension of Love

Letter 1: "The Divine Spark - Our Love's Spiritual Connection"
Letter 2: "The Sacred Covenant - Our Love's Divine Promise"
Letter 3: "The Love's Prayer - Our Shared Spiritual Hope" Letter 4: "The Holy Bond - The Sanctity of Our Love"
Letter 5: "The Spiritual Oasis - Our Love's Divine Refuge"

Chapter 7: Letter 1: The Divine Spark – Our Love's Spiritual Connection

My Beloved,

Words fail to fully capture the depth and significance of the spiritual connection we share. You are not only my lifelong partner but also my soulmate and spiritual companion. In this letter, I want to express my heartfelt thankfulness to God for the divine spark that ignites and sustains our love.

From the very beginning, I knew that our union was not merely coincidental but divinely orchestrated. Our love is a testament to God's perfect plan and His faithfulness in granting my prayers for a partner according to His will. You embody all the qualities I prayed for and more, and I am humbled by the gift of your presence in my life.

Our spiritual connection goes beyond the physical realm. It is a bond that intertwines our souls, drawing strength and inspiration from our shared faith. The spiritual dimension of our love adds a sacred depth to our relationship, infusing every moment with a sense of purpose and divine alignment.

In your presence, I feel a profound sense of peace and spiritual alignment. Our shared beliefs, values, and devotion to our Savior serve as a guiding light, illuminating our path together. Our love is rooted in the sanctity of God's love and the eternal promises found in His Word.

This spiritual connection grants us hope, comfort, and strength in the face of life's challenges. We find solace in prayer, seeking divine guidance, and surrendering our fears and worries to the loving hands of our Heavenly Father. It is through our spiritual unity that we weather storms and find renewed hope in His promises.

As we journey together, my love, let us continue to nurture and deepen our spiritual connection. May we always prioritize the sacred dimension of our love, cherishing the moments of prayer, worship, and spiritual growth. Let our love be a testament to the power of God's love working within us, drawing us closer to Him and each other.

I am immensely grateful for the divine spark that unites us, for it is in this spiritual connection that I find immeasurable joy and fulfillment. Your unshakeable faith, love, and understanding are a constant source of inspiration and encouragement. Our love is a reflection of God's love for us, and I am honored to walk this sacred journey with you.

With all my love and devotion,
[Your Name]

Chapter 7: Letter 2: The Sacred Covenant – Our Love's Divine Promise

My Beloved [Spouse's Name],

As I reflect upon the sacred covenant we share, I am grateful to the Lord for the divine promise that binds our love together. Our journey as husband and wife is not merely a union of two souls, but a testament to the divine grace and guidance that has brought us together.

In a world where relationships often falter and fade, our love stands as a beacon of hope and steadfastness. It is a love rooted in the sacred covenant we made before the Lord, promising to honor and cherish one another through all the seasons of life.

The sacred covenant we entered into is not to be taken lightly. It is a promise that goes beyond our individual desires and preferences. It is a commitment to seek the Lord first and to align our lives with His divine will. As we place our trust in Him, our love is enriched and transformed into something truly remarkable.

I am reminded of the words spoken in Matthew 6:33, "But seek first the kingdom of God and his righteousness, and all these things will be added to you." This verse holds a profound truth for our relationship. When we prioritize our relationship with the Lord, He pours out His blessings upon us and guides our steps on this beautiful journey together.

Beloved, I want you to know that my love for you is not based on fleeting emotions or circumstances. It is a love deeply rooted in the sacred covenant we made, and it is a love that is unwavering and enduring. Through the highs and lows, the joys and challenges, I promise to stand by your side, honoring our divine promise with all my heart.

Our love is a testament to the transformative power of the sacred covenant. It is through our commitment to seek the Lord first that we discover the true meaning and purpose of life. In each other's arms, we find comfort, support, and an unshakeable bond that strengthens us.

As we continue our journey together, let us hold fast to the sacred covenant we made. Let us daily seek the Lord's guidance and wisdom, allowing His love to flow through us and radiate to those around us. May our love be a testimony of the divine promise that awaits those who place their trust in Him.

I love you deeply and wholeheartedly, my beloved. May our love always be a reflection of the sacred covenant we share, and may the Lord's blessings continue to abound in our lives.

Forever yours,
[Your Name]

Chapter 7: Letter 3: The Love's Prayer – Our Shared Spiritual Hope

My Dearest [Spouse's Name],

As I pour out my heart in this love's prayer, I am rejoicing in the spiritual hope we share. Our love is not simply a product of our own strength or efforts; it is a divine gift, a reflection of the transformative power of prayer and the presence of the Lord in our lives.

In the solitude of my thoughts, I am reminded of the profound impact prayer has had on our relationship. It is through prayer that our hearts have been softened, our spirits have been renewed, and our love has been deepened. Prayer is the foundation upon which our love stands, connecting us to each other and to the Lord in a way that is both humbling and awe-inspiring.

The beauty of prayer lies in its ability to bring us into the presence of God, to open our hearts and minds to His will. It is in these moments of quiet reflection that we find solace, guidance, and a deepening understanding of the depths of our love.

As I meditate on the words of Romans 12:12, "Be joyful in hope, patient in affliction, faithful in prayer," I am reminded of the power of hope and faith in our lives. Through prayer, we find the strength to persevere through challenges, the courage to face the unknown, and the assurance that the Lord is always by our side.

Beloved, our shared spiritual hope is a precious gift that sets us apart. It is through prayer that we invite the presence of the Lord into our relationship, surrendering our desires, fears, and dreams to His perfect will. In the act of praying together, we are not only drawn closer to Him but also to each other, creating an unbreakable bond rooted in faith and trust.

Through prayer, we are transformed. It is in those moments of vulnerability and surrender that we experience the true depth of love and the power of the Holy Spirit working within us. Prayer allows us to see each other through the eyes of God, to love unconditionally, and to extend grace and forgiveness.

As we continue on this journey of faith, may our love's prayer be a testament to the hope we have in the Lord. May it be a beacon of light to those around us, inspiring them to seek the transformative power of prayer in their own lives. Let us always remember that our love is not merely a human endeavor, but a divine connection that points to the love and grace of our Savior.

With each prayer we offer together, my heart is filled with a deep sense of joy for the gift of you. I cherish the moments of reflection and communion we share, knowing that in prayer, we are forever united in love and hope.

Yours eternally,
[Your Name]

Chapter 7: Letter 4: The Holy Bond – The Sanctity of Our Love

My Beloved [Spouse's Name],

As I write this letter, my humble heart is thankful for the holy bond we share and the sanctity of our love. Our connection is not merely a human union but a divine gift bestowed upon us by the grace of our Lord Jesus Christ. In the face of life's challenges and uncertainties, our love stands strong, guided by our shared faith and unshakeable trust in the goodness of God.

The sanctity of our love lies in the knowledge that we are not alone in this journey. We are yoked together, not only with each other but also with the Almighty. Our bond is rooted in our shared spiritual walk, as we strive to align our hearts and minds with His perfect will.

As I reflect on the words of 2 Corinthians 6:14, "Do not be unequally yoked with unbelievers. For what partnership has righteousness with lawlessness? Or what fellowship has light with darkness?" I am reminded of the importance of being equally yoked in our faith. Our mutual dedication to our Lord has strengthened the foundation of our love, allowing it to flourish in ways that surpass the limitations of this world.

Beloved, our love is not immune to the challenges of life. We have faced trials and tribulations, and yet through it all, the peace of the Lord has sustained us. It is in the depths of our shared spiritual journey that we find solace, strength, and unwavering hope. The sanctity of our love allows us to face life's storms with grace, knowing that we are anchored in the steadfast love of our Savior.

The Lord's goodness has been evident in every aspect of our relationship. It is His presence in our lives that fuels the fire of our love, igniting a passion and affection that transcends the ordinary. It is through His grace that we find forgiveness, compassion, and the ability to love each other unconditionally.

Beloved, I am in awe of the way our love has grown and flourished in the sanctuary of our shared faith. It is in the sacred moments of prayer, worship, and devotion that we have witnessed the transformative power of God's love working within us. He has molded our hearts, allowing us to become vessels of His love and instruments of His peace.

As we continue on this journey of faith, may the sanctity of our love serve as a beacon of hope to those around us. May our union be a testament to the power of God's grace, as we demonstrate the depth of His love through our love for one another. Let us cherish the holy bond we share, for it is a precious gift that reflects the divine nature of our Creator.

Chapter 7: Letter 4: The Holy Bond – The Sanctity of Our Love (cont.)

In your arms, my love, I find comfort and security, knowing that our love is not merely a human connection but a sacred covenant. I thank the Lord every day for the blessing of your love and for the joy and peace that it brings to my life. Together, let us continue to walk this path of faith, holding fast to the sanctity of our love.

Yours always,
[Your Name]

Chapter 7: Letter 5: The Spiritual Oasis – A Divine Refuge

My Dearest [Spouse's Name],

As I write this letter, I feel a well springing up into a spiritual oasis in which we find our love. Our relationship is not just a bond between two souls, but a divine refuge, a sanctuary where we find solace, strength, and unbreakable devotion.

In the depths of our connection, I am reminded of the words of Psalm 62:8, "Trust in him at all times, you people; pour out your hearts to him, for God is our refuge." Our love is a reflection of the divine refuge we have found in the arms of our Lord Jesus Christ. It is through His love that we are able to love one another deeply, unconditionally, and selflessly.

Beloved, I am privileged to walk this journey of faith with you. You are not just my partner, my soulmate, but my spiritual oasis. In your presence, I find peace, serenity, and a love that transcends the boundaries of this world. Together, we have discovered a connection that is rooted in the love of our Savior.

Our love is not of this world alone; it is infused with the love that is divine. It is a love that goes beyond human comprehension, a love that is patient, kind, and forgiving. It is a love that seeks the best for one another and finds joy in the growth of our spirits.

In this spiritual oasis we have cultivated, we find refuge from the chaos of the world. It is a place where we can retreat, seeking the face of our Lord, and finding renewal and strength in His presence. It is through this divine refuge that our love is sustained and our spirits are refreshed.

Beloved, I am grateful for the spiritual oasis we share, where we can pour out our hearts, our hopes, and our dreams before the Lord. It is in this sacred space that we find guidance, wisdom, and a deepening of our faith. Together, we navigate life's challenges, knowing that our love is anchored in the rock of our salvation.

As I reflect on our journey, I am reminded of the beautiful verse in Song of Solomon 4:12, "A garden enclosed is my sister, my spouse; a spring shut up, a fountain sealed." Our love is a garden enclosed, a place of intimacy and connection that is cherished and protected. It is a fountain of joy, a wellspring of hope that flows endlessly as we draw closer to our Savior.

Beloved, thank you for being my spiritual oasis, my refuge in times of trial and my source of strength. I am in awe of the depth of our love and the divine connection we share. Let us continue to nurture and cultivate this spiritual oasis, knowing that our love is a reflection of the love our Lord has for us.

With all my heart,
[Your Name]

Chapter 7: Letter 6: The Divine Tapestry – Weaving Our Love with Faith

My Dearest [Spouse's Name],

As I contemplate the intricate tapestry of our love, I am filled with awe and gratitude for the divine threads that weave through our lives. Our love, intertwined with faith, forms a masterpiece beyond imagination, a love that is both profound and transcendent.

In the tapestry of our love, I see the fingerprints of God, the divine artist who skillfully weaves the threads of faith into the fabric of our relationship. It is through our shared belief and trust in Him that our love flourishes and grows, reaching heights we could never have imagined.

Beloved, our love is more than a mere human connection; it is a sacred bond infused with the light of faith. It is a love that is guided by divine providence, directed by the gentle hand of our Heavenly Father. As we surrender ourselves to His will, our love becomes an extraordinary work of art, a reflection of His grace and mercy.

Just as a tapestry is comprised of various threads, each with its unique color and texture, our love is enriched by the diversity of our experiences, our personalities, and our individual walks of faith. Together, we create a tapestry that is vibrant, harmonious, and filled with depth.

In the tapestry of our love, I see the promises of God interwoven with our hopes and dreams. His Word reminds us in Hebrews 11:1 that "faith is the assurance of things hoped for, the conviction of things not seen." It is our faith, dear one that allows us to envision a love that surpasses the boundaries of this world, a love that transcends time and space.

As we navigate the tapestry of life, I am in awe of the way our love is strengthened and refined by the challenges we face. Just as a tapestry becomes more beautiful with each thread woven into its fabric, our love becomes more resilient with every trial we overcome. It is through our faith that we find the courage to persevere, to face the unknown hand in hand.

Beloved, I am forever grateful for the divine tapestry that is our love. It is a tapestry that speaks of sacrifice, forgiveness, and unconditional devotion. It is a testament to the power of faith, which enables us to love one another with a depth and intensity that is beyond comprehension.

As we continue to weave our love with faith, let us embrace the beauty of the unknown, knowing that our Heavenly Father is the master weaver, orchestrating every stitch with His perfect wisdom and love. Together, we create a tapestry that reflects His glory, a tapestry that bears witness to the incredible love we share.

With a heart full of love,
[Your Name]

Chapter 7: Letter 7: The Love's Scripture – Our Spiritual Guide

My Dearest [Spouse's Name],

As I reflect on the journey of our love, I am reminded of the profound impact that love scriptures have had on our lives. They serve as a guiding light, leading us towards a deeper spiritual connection and an unwavering faith in the Lord.

In the early days of our marriage, I confess that I was hesitant to fully embrace the spiritual walk. I had not yet realized the transformative power that inviting Jesus into our hearts would have on our relationship. But as we opened our hearts to Him and allowed Him to work within us, a beautiful change began to unfold.

Beloved, I am filled with both remorse and gratitude. Remorse for the times when I may have been closed off to the spiritual journey we were meant to embark on together. Gratitude for the divine grace that has transformed our hearts and our lives.

The love scriptures, rooted in the Word of God, have become our spiritual guide. They illuminate our path and provide the wisdom and comfort we need in every season of life. As we meditate on these verses, they reveal profound truths that guide us towards a love that is selfless, patient, and enduring.

One such scripture that has deeply resonated with me is 1 Corinthians 13:4-7, which reminds us that "Love is patient, love is kind. It does not envy, it does not boast, it is not proud. It does not dishonor others, it is not self-seeking, it is not easily angered, it keeps no record of wrongs. Love does not delight in evil but rejoices with the truth. It always protects, always trusts, always hopes, always perseveres."

These words, my love, serve as a compass, directing us towards a love that reflects the heart of our Savior. They teach us to be patient and kind, to let go of pride and selfishness, and to forgive and seek forgiveness. They remind us to protect and trust one another, to hold onto hope even in the face of challenges, and to persevere in our love.

As we allow the love scriptures to shape our hearts and guide our actions, we witness the miraculous transformation that takes place. Our love becomes a reflection of God's love, a love that is unshakeable, unending, and filled with grace.

Beloved, I am deeply grateful for the spiritual guide that the love scriptures provide us. They lead us on a path of righteousness and inspire us to live out our faith in every aspect of our lives. As we continue to immerse ourselves in the Word of God, our love will continue to blossom and flourish, creating a beautiful testimony of His goodness and grace.

With all my love,
[Your Name]

Chapter 7: Letter 8: The Sacred Garden – Cultivating Our Spiritual Love

My Dearest [Spouse's Name],

As I wander through the garden of our love, I am captivated by the sacredness that fills the air. Our love is like a flourishing garden, cultivated by the tender care of our Savior, where our spiritual love blooms in abundance.

In this sacred garden, we find a love that goes beyond human comprehension. It is a love that is rooted in the unconditional and selfless nature of our Savior, the Lord Jesus Christ. As we immerse ourselves in His words, we witness the transformation of our hearts, where our own self-serving beliefs and desires are pushed aside, and making room for the pure and overflowing love of God.

One scripture that speaks to the depth of our spiritual love is found in 1 John 4:7-8, which proclaims, "Beloved, let us love one another, for love is from God, and whoever loves has been born of God and knows God. Anyone who does not love does not know God, because God is love."

These words remind us that our love is not merely a human emotion but a divine reflection of the nature of our Creator. It is through His love that we find fulfillment and purpose. The more we fill our lives with God's presence and His Holy Spirit, the more our love overflows and pours into the lives of others.

Beloved, as we cultivate our spiritual love, we discover great joy and fulfillment. Our love becomes a beacon of hope and light in a world that so desperately needs it. It is through our love that we fulfill the purpose God has ordained for each one of us, to spread His love and grace to all those we encounter.

In this sacred garden of our love, I am humbled by the magnitude of Christ's love that flows through us. I am grateful for the depth of our spiritual connection, knowing that it is a gift from our Heavenly Father. It is this love that binds us together and allows us to weather any storm that comes our way.

Beloved, let us continue to nurture and cultivate this sacred garden of our love. As we surrender ourselves to God's will, His love will continue to flourish within us, and our love will be a testimony to His grace and goodness. Together, we will continue to grow in our spiritual journey, hand in hand, as we experience the beauty and abundance of a love that is rooted in the Divine.

With all my love,
[Your Name]

Chapter 7: Letter 9: The Whole Union – Our Love's Sacred Joining

My Dearest [Spouse's Name],

As I reflect on the sacred joining of our love, I am humbly amazed at the unbreakable bond we share. Our love is not merely a union of two hearts but a holy union, woven together by the divine presence of our Lord Jesus Christ.

In the book of Matthew 19:6, Jesus affirms the sanctity of marriage, saying, "So they are no longer two but one flesh. What therefore God has joined together, let not man separate." This scripture reminds us that our love is not just a human connection but a sacred joining blessed by God Himself.

I am deeply thankful to the Lord for answering my prayers and granting me a spouse who loves Him as deeply as I do. Our shared devotion to the Lord has become the cornerstone of our relationship, allowing us to walk together in faith, hand in hand. It is in this holy union that we experience the fullness of God's love and grace.

Beloved, the experiences we share in this sacred union are on a different level. As we journey together, we have the privilege of encountering the living God, the Holy Spirit, who dwells within us. Our love transcends the ordinary and touches the extraordinary because it is infused with the divine presence of God Himself.

I am humbled by the depth of our connection and the blessings that flow from it. Our love is not confined to the boundaries of this world but is rooted in eternity. It is a love that brings us joy, peace, and a sense of purpose beyond measure.

In this whole union of our love, I am reminded of the words in Song of Solomon 8:7, "Many waters cannot quench love; rivers cannot sweep it away" This verse beautifully captures the enduring and unyielding nature of our love. Just as no waters can extinguish a flame, nothing can diminish the love we share.

Beloved, let us continue to cherish and nurture this sacred joining of our love. As we walk hand in hand, guided by our shared faith, we can face any challenge that comes our way. Our love is a testament to God's goodness and grace, and I am forever grateful for the blessing of having you as my partner in this divine journey.

With all my love,
[Your Name]

Chapter 7: Letter 10: The Faith's Bridge – Connecting Our Love and Belief

My Dearest [Spouse's Name],

I love you so much and I love this journey of faith we are on together, my heart is so happy we can share this divine connection. Our love is not bound by earthly limits but is elevated by the bridge of faith that connects our hearts and beliefs.

In the book of Hebrews 11:1, it is written, "Now faith is the assurance of things hoped for, the conviction of things not seen." Our love is rooted in this faith, a deep trust in the unseen and a hope that surpasses human understanding. It is through our shared belief in Jesus Christ, the Alpha and Omega, the one who sits on the throne, that our love finds its true purpose and meaning.

Beloved, when we open our hearts to Jesus, allowing Him to work within us, something extraordinary happens. He takes residence in our souls, transforming us from within. His love, His joy, His peace, and all the wonderful attributes of Christ begin to flow through us, connecting us in a way that surpasses our human understanding.

In this divine connection of love and belief, we experience a profound oneness. Our hearts beat in rhythm with the heartbeat of our Savior. We find solace and strength in His presence, knowing that He walks with us through every season of life.

As we journey together, hand in hand, I pray that our love will always be a reflection of God's grace and goodness.
May we continue to seek Him first in all that we do, trusting in His unfailing love to guide us.

Beloved, I offer this prayer from the depths of my heart: May the Lord bless you and protect you. May He make His face shine upon you and be gracious to you. May He turn His face toward you and grant you His peace. May our love be a testament to His faithfulness and a beacon of hope to others.

Thank you for joining me on this incredible journey of faith, love, and belief. Our connection is sacred, and I am forever grateful for the gift of your presence in my life. Let us continue to walk in faith, hand in hand, as we embrace the love that transcends all understanding.

With all my love and prayers,
[Your Name]

LETTER TO MY FATHER

My Dearest Lord Jesus Christ,

Words cannot express the depth of gratitude and love that fills my heart as I pour out my adoration to You my sweet and amazing Papa. You are the center of my being, the reason for my existence, and I am forever indebted to Your grace and mercy.

Thank You, Lord, for choosing me, for predestining me to be Yours. I am humbled and honored to be called Your beloved. Without You, I would have been lost, wandering aimlessly in the darkness. But You, in Your infinite wisdom, found me, rescued me, and brought me into the light of Your love.

I bow before You, my Savior, and I surrender my heart to Your perfect will. You gave me the freedom to choose, and I am eternally grateful that I said, "Yes, Lord, I am Yours." My life is forever changed because of Your redeeming love and sacrifice on the cross. You bore the weight of my sins, and through Your death and resurrection, You granted me eternal life and a restored relationship with You.

Lord, I cannot fathom walking through this journey of life without You by my side. You are my everything, my refuge, and my strength. In Your presence, I find solace, comfort, and unwavering love. I am forever Yours, and my heart rejoices at the thought of being in Your loving embrace.

I thank You, Lord, for blessing me with a wonderful husband, Brad, who shares in this incredible journey with me. Together, we desire to be a reflection of Your perfect love and unity. May our lives exhibit Your divine purpose, shining Your light into the lives of those we encounter. Guide us, Lord, in our relationship, that we may be a testament to Your grace and a source of encouragement and love to others.

Lord, I pray that You continue to speak to us, to reveal Yourself more deeply, and to open our hearts to hear Your voice. Give us obedient and submissive spirits, that we may follow You wholeheartedly and walk in the path You have set before us. We long to be vessels of Your love, channels of Your blessings, and instruments of Your peace.

Thank You, Lord, for everything You have done and continue to do in my life. I love You more than words can express, and I am forever grateful for Your unending love and faithfulness.

In Your Precious and Holy name, I pray. Amen.

Your devoted daughter,
Sylwia

Conclusion

As we come to the end of "Letters of Love," let these heartfelt words echo in our hearts and minds. They remind us of the profound connection between our love for one another and our unwavering faith in our Lord Jesus Christ. Through the ups and downs, the challenges and triumphs, our love has been anchored in the unwavering presence of our Savior.

Throughout this book, we have embarked on a heartfelt journey, exploring the depths and dimensions of love. We celebrated the sanctity of love, the resilience it brings, and the transformative power it holds. Each chapter revealed a unique aspect of love's journey, intertwining with faith and guiding us towards a profound understanding of its significance.

From the first blooming of love's awakening to the deepening bonds and the tests of resilience, we witnessed the beauty of commitment and the strength that love can provide. We navigated challenges together, recognizing that love is not without its trials but that it has the power to endure and grow stronger in the face of adversity.

In the exploration of devotion, we discovered the depth and sacredness of our love, rooted in a spiritual connection with our Lord. We found solace in prayer, guidance in scripture, and the unbreakable union that faith brings to our relationship.

As we bid farewell to "Letters of Love," let these words continue to resonate in our hearts. Carry the lessons learned, the moments cherished, and the guidance offered into your own journey of love and faith. May your love be a testament to the transformative power of faith and the profound depths that love can reach.

Remember that love is a gift to be cherished, nurtured, and celebrated. It is through the divine dimension of love, rooted in faith, that we find strength, resilience, and joy. Embrace the journey of love with an open heart, knowing that with faith in Jesus Christ, all things are possible. Let your love be a reflection of God's love for you, radiating His light and sharing His blessings with others.

In closing, may your love be a beautiful symphony, blending the melodies of faith, commitment, and devotion. May it be a beacon of light and hope in a world that longs for genuine love. May your journey be filled with joy, peace, and an ever-deepening connection with your beloved and with our loving Father, who blesses and guides us in our pursuit of love.

With heartfelt blessings and the assurance of the divine,
In Jesus Precious Name
Sylwia Mills

Acknowledgments

First and foremost, I would like to express my deepest gratitude to our, God and Savior Lord Jesus Christ, whose love and grace have been the foundation of this book. Your presence and guidance have infused every word, every letter with meaning and purpose. Thank you for inspiring me to write and for blessing this project.

Thank You for Your love, Your grace, and Your provision throughout the entire process of writing and publishing this book. I am humbled and honored to have had the opportunity to share these letters with the world, and I pray that they serve as a reminder of the beauty and transformative power of love and faith.

To my beloved husband, Brad, you have been my constant source of love, support, and inspiration. Your unwavering faith and your golden heart have fueled the creation of "Letters of Love." Thank you for being the inspiration behind this book, for walking this journey of love and faith with me, and for being my partner, my soulmate, my spiritmate in all aspects of life.

I would like to extend my heartfelt appreciation to my family and friends who have supported me throughout this writing process. Your encouragement, love, and belief in me have been invaluable. Thank you for being my cheerleaders, my sounding boards, and my pillars of strength.

I also would like to express my heartfelt gratitude to the following individuals, who have played an integral role in my spiritual journey and have had a profound impact on my relationship with our Lord. Each of them holds a special place in my heart, and their guidance, encouragement, and unwavering faith have been instrumental in shaping my path: Margaret Slipko, Gloria Valencia, Dawn Buford, and Jan Caballero-Ding, Daniel Fantell, Brother Ron (my spiritual father).

Your presence in my life and your unwavering support have been a true blessing. As I embarked on this journey of walking with the Lord, your shepherding and steadfast faith have uplifted and inspired me. Your guidance and encouragement have been like a guiding light, illuminating my path and filling my heart with strength and conviction.

I am incredibly grateful for the love, support, and wisdom you have shared with me. Your belief in me and your unwavering faith in our Lord have propelled me forward, even during challenging times. Your impact on my spiritual growth cannot be overstated, and I am truly blessed to call you my friends and spiritual warriors. Thank you for being a significant part of my journey, for your love, and for your unwavering support. May the Lord continue to guide and bless you abundantly as you walk in His light.

To my editor and the publishing team, thank you for your guidance, expertise, and dedication in helping me bring this book to life. Your invaluable contributions have shaped and refined the letters within these pages. I am grateful for your professionalism and unwavering commitment to excellence.

Finally, I want to express my deepest gratitude to all the readers who have embarked on this journey through "Letters of Love," thank you for your time and willingness to immerse yourselves in these heartfelt expressions of love. It is my sincerest hope that these letters touch your hearts, inspire you to cherish and celebrate love, and encourage you to share your own love through the power of written words.

Much Love to You,
Sylwia Mills